"What kind of vibe from me are you getting?" he asked.

"One that makes me wonder how often you get involved with women who are part of a case you're working on."

"Never." He continued holding her gaze. "But there's a first time for everything, with the right woman."

She looked away, lamplight playing across the curve of her cheek and the smooth column of her neck. He fought the urge to kiss her there.

"This may be the definition of bad timing," she said.

"Probably," he said.

"But do I feel this attraction to you because there's something between us, or because you're something steady I can hold on to while I'm reeling from my sister's disappearance?"

"I think the only way we're going to learn the answer to that question is to stick around and find out," he said.

D1534612

MANHUNT ON MYSTIC MESA

Cindi Myers

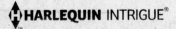

For Denise, the best sister-in-law ever.

Recycling programs for this product may not exist in your area.

ISBN-13: 978-0-373-75694-0

Manhunt on Mystic Mesa

Copyright © 2017 by Cynthia Myers

Printed in U.S.A.

CAST OF CHARACTERS

Ryan Spencer—The newest member of the Ranger Brigade has a talent for investigation and is determined to find the man responsible for the disappearance of three women. But his attraction to the sister of one victim may distract him from his job—or lead him to the guilty party.

Jana Lassiter—The quiet, controlled CPA will do anything to find her missing sister, including working with the sexy investigator who alternately comforts her and rubs her the wrong way. This has to be the worst timing in the world for a relationship, but around Ryan Spencer, her emotions are out of control.

Jenny Lassiter—The nineteen-year-old college student disappeared from a remote archaeological dig. Investigations reveal she had a secret life that included juggling two romances. Did struggles in her personal life or something on the job lead to her disappearance?

Daniel Metwater—The leader of a wandering band of back-to-nature spiritualists has a reputation as a ladies' man and a habit of lying to the Ranger Brigade. Is it only coincidence that all the missing women disappeared near his camp?

Jerome Eddleston—The married archaeology professor's affair with Jenny Lassiter may not be the only secret he was keeping from his wealthy wife. Was his breakup with Jenny as peaceful as he portrays?

Eric Patterson—The cocky newspaper reporter claims to be Jenny's closest friend, but some elements of his story don't add up.

Cindi Myers is the author of more than fifty novels. When she's not crafting new romance plots, she enjoys skiing, gardening, cooking, crafting and daydreaming. A lover of small-town life, she lives with her husband and two spoiled dogs in the Colorado mountains.

Books by Cindi Myers

Harlequin Intrigue

The Ranger Brigade: Family Secrets

Murder in Black Canyon
Undercover Husband
Manhunt on Mystic Mesa

The Men of Search Team Seven

Colorado Crime Scene
Lawman on the Hunt
Christmas Kidnapping
PhD Protector

The Ranger Brigade

The Guardian
Lawman Protection
Colorado Bodyguard
Black Canyon Conspiracy

Rocky Mountain Revenge
Rocky Mountain Rescue

Visit the Author Profile page at Harlequin.com for more titles.

Chapter One

"We've got another missing woman." Commander Graham Ellison tossed the photo of a smiling blonde in the middle of the table where the members of the Ranger Brigade had gathered for a morning briefing. The fresh-faced, blue-eyed young woman radiated vitality and happiness, jarring when compared to the stony visage of the commander. "Her name is Jennifer Lassiter, nineteen years old, from Denver," Ellison continued. "She was one of a group of archaeology students working in the area."

"That makes two missing women in the past month." One of the officers seated around the table—the only woman, whose nametag identified her as Carmen Redhorse—glanced at the photo and passed it down the table.

"Three." Officer Ryan Spencer spoke from the doorway of the room. The rest of the team swiveled to stare at him. Not exactly the entrance he had wanted to make on his first day at his new job. He ignored the stares, strode to the table and pulled out the only empty chair, at the end opposite the commander.

"Who are you?" a sharp-nosed, lean man who sat behind an open laptop—Simon Woolridge—demanded.

"This is Ryan Spencer, with Customs and Border Protection," Commander Ellison said. "Our newest team member."

Ryan sat. "Sorry I'm late," he said. The drive from Montrose had taken longer than he had anticipated, partly because he had gotten behind a caravan of RVs making their way into Black Canyon of the Gunnison National Park, where the Ranger Brigade task force's headquarters were located. But he didn't bother to mention that. As his dad had always told him—never make excuses.

"What do you mean three women are missing instead of two?" The man to the commander's left spoke. He was the picture of a rugged outdoorsman—dark eyes and hair, olive skin, a hawk nose and strong chin. His nametag read Michael Dance.

"I got a bulletin this morning from my office," Ryan said. "My former office." Though he was technically still an officer with United

States Customs and Border Protection, Ryan's current assignment made him a member of the multiagency task force whose job it was to prevent and solve crime on the vast network of public lands in southwestern Colorado.

He took out his phone and pulled up the message. "Her name is Alicia Mendoza and she's from Guatemala. Part of a group of illegal immigrants who were traveling through this area on their way to work in Utah. When they were picked up last night, one of them reported that Alicia had disappeared two days ago, near the national park."

Simon snorted. "Nice of them to let us know."

"You know now." Ryan pocketed his phone and looked around the table.

"Don't mind Simon." The man on Ryan's left offered his hand. "He's our resident grouch. I'm Randall Knightbridge. BLM."

"Pleased to meet you." Ryan shook hands with the Bureau of Land Management ranger, then turned to the man on his right.

"Ethan Reynolds," the man said. "I'm new, too. Only been with the Rangers a couple of months. I came over from the FBI."

"We'll finish the introductions later." The commander consulted a sheaf of papers in his hand. "Back to the matter of the three missing women. Jennifer Lassiter's fellow archaeology students report that she took a break early yesterday afternoon. A little while later, they noticed she was missing. Her friends searched the area for several hours but could find no sign of her. They notified park rangers and the county sheriff, who brought us in this morning."

"Where was she last seen?" Simon asked.

"Out near Mystic Mesa," the commander said. "The group is excavating an early Native American settlement."

"Daniel Metwater and his bunch are camped near there, aren't they?" Randall asked.

"They are." Simon tapped a few keys on the laptop. "They just received a new permit to camp near a spring out there. Their permit for their site near Coyote Creek expired last week."

"After the prairie fire they set near there, I'm surprised the park service renewed their permit," the woman said.

"The fire they allegedly set," a tall Hispanic officer who sat at the commander's right—Marco Cruz—said. "Fire investigators determined the wildfire was human-caused, but they have no proof anyone from Metwater's group was responsible."

"Except we know they were," Simon said.

Ethan leaned toward Ryan. "Daniel Metwater is a self-styled prophet who leads a band of followers around the wilderness," he explained. "There has been a lot of suspicious activity associated with his bunch, but we haven't been able to pin anything on him."

"The first young woman who went missing, Lucia Raton, was in Metwater's camp shortly before she disappeared," the commander said. "At first, he denied knowing her, but later we confirmed she had been in camp. She wanted to join his group, but he says he sent her away because she was underage."

"Later, we found a necklace that belonged to her buried about a mile from the camp, with a lot of things belonging to one of Metwater's 'family' members," the woman said.

"No body has been found and her family hasn't heard from her," Randall concluded.

"Interesting that this latest missing woman disappeared near Metwater's camp." Ethan tapped his pen on the conference table. "Where did the Guatemalan woman disappear?"

Ryan consulted his phone again. "It just says in the Curecanti National Recreation Area."

"That's forty-three thousand acres," Simon said. "You'll need to narrow it down a little."

"See if you can get some more specifics," the commander said. "Then you and Ethan follow up with the archaeologists, see what you can find out about Jennifer Lassiter."

"Maybe she got tired of digging in the dirt and decided to take a vacation with a boyfriend," Michael Dance said.

"For her sake, I hope that's the story," Carmen said.

"Moving on." The commander consulted his notes. "Lance, any update on the plant-smuggling case?"

Simon smothered what sounded like a laugh.

"What kind of plants?" Ryan asked.

"Expensive ones." Lance, a lanky young man, leaned back in his chair to address them. "The park rangers have found several places where the thief is digging up ornamental plants, some of which retail for hundreds of dollars. We've got a few faint tire tracks, but there's nothing distinct about them. No witnesses. Unless we catch this guy in the act, I don't think we have much of a chance."

"All right," the commander said. "We're almost done here. Just a little housekeeping to take care of." Ryan's mind wandered as Ellison shared some bulletins from area law enforcement, a heads-up about a controlled burn the Forest Service was conducting in the area, and construction updates in the park. The Ranger Brigade was an unusual force, comprised of officers from many different agencies, tasked with overseeing an expanse of public land the size of Indiana. Only a few hundred people occupied that land, but the potential for criminal activity, from smuggling to manufacturing drugs to theft of public property, was huge.

"All right, you're dismissed," Commander Ellison said. "Have a safe day."

Ryan pulled out his phone and sent a text to his former supervisor at Customs and Border Protection, asking for the specific location where Alicia Mendoza had been last seen. He hit the send button as the female officer approached. Her straight black hair hung almost to her waist, and her tawny skin and high cheekbones attested to a Native American heritage. "I'm Carmen Redhorse," she said. "Welcome to the team."

"Simon Woolridge." The agent with the laptop shook hands also. "I'm the tech expert on the squad. I've got lots of information on Daniel Metwater, if you need it."

"I'm Marco Cruz, DEA." The Hispanic agent from the Drug Enforcement Agency had a grip of steel, but a welcoming expression. "I hope you like working in the great outdoors, because we've got a lot of territory we cover, most of it pretty empty."

"Things can get exciting, though." Randall Knightbridge joined them, a cup of coffee in one hand, a fawn-and-black police dog at his side. "This is Lotte," he introduced the dog. "Another member of the team."

The last two officers he would be working with introduced themselves—Michael Dance was the rugged outdoorsman who had been seated at the other end of the conference table, and Lance Carpenter was the Montrose County Sheriff's Deputy who was heading up the stolen-plant investigation.

"Are you married?" Marco asked.

"No. The job hasn't given me much time for girlfriends."

"You might be surprised," Marco said. "But if you're not interested in a relationship, you might want to avoid drinking the water around here."

The others laughed, and, at Ryan's confused look, Randall said, "A lot of us have gotten engaged or married recently. It's starting to look like it's contagious."

"But some of us are still immune," Simon said.

"Thanks for the warning," Ryan said. "I

think." He hadn't come to the Rangers to find romance, but to jump-start a career that was beginning to feel stale.

Ethan clapped Ryan on the back. "Ready to talk to the archaeologists?" he asked.

"I am," Ryan said, grateful to have the conversation focused on the job once more. "Where are they located from here?"

"Come here and I'll show you." Ethan led the way to a map that took up much of one wall of the headquarters building. "We're here." He pointed to the national park entrance, then traced a path northeast to a flattened ridge. "And this is Mystic Mesa. The archaeologists have been excavating on the eastern side of the Mesa."

Randall, who had followed them, pointed to a draw Ryan guessed was about a mile from the archaeology dig. "Daniel Metwater and his followers are camped in here," he said.

"A prophet and his followers in the wilderness." Ryan shook his head. "That sounds so—I don't know—Old Testament."

"He isn't that kind of prophet," Randall said.

"What do you mean?" Ryan asked.

"No beard or robe in sight," Randall said. "He's the son of a wealthy industrialist and supposedly inherited the family fortune. Most of his followers are young people, searching for something."

"A lot of them are really beautiful young women," Ethan said.

"So you think he's killing some of them?" Ryan asked. "But it doesn't sound like the women who disappeared were part of his group."

"They weren't, but we know that at least one of them—Lucia Raton—had expressed an interest in Metwater's writings," Ethan said. "And it's a weird coincidence that she and Jennifer Lassiter were last seen near his camp."

Ryan's phone vibrated and he glanced at the screen. "This says Alicia Mendoza disappeared when the group she was traveling with stopped for water at a spring at the base of a mesa that ran north-south," he said. "The people she was traveling with didn't know a name and couldn't be more precise than that."

"Mystic Mesa runs north-south," Randall said. He pointed to a spot on the map. "And there's a spring right at the base of it. The only one for miles."

"That's only a stone's throw from Metwater's camp," Ethan said.

"Too much of a coincidence," Ryan said.

"Then I guess you know who else you need to talk to." Randall clapped Ryan on the shoulder. "Have fun," he said. "Metwater may or may not be a murderer, but he's definitely a pain in the backside."

JANA LASSITER GRIPPED the steering wheel of her Jeep and studied the barren landscape where her sister, Jenny, had disappeared. Red-rock chimneys and hoodoos jutted up from a flat plain of yellowed bunchgrass and dusty green piñon trees, their soot-gray trunks stunted and gnarled from years of fighting harsh winds and scorching sun. Dry washes and deeper canyons made fissures in the dusty surface of the land. Jenny had texted that she loved this place—that the remoteness and wildness of it made her feel so free. But the vast emptiness put Jana on edge. Compared to this great expanse, a single human was insignificant. With no signposts or roads or buildings, she already felt lost. Was that what had happened to Jenny? Had she wandered away from her group and simply forgotten where she was? Or had something more sinister taken her away?

Fighting a feeling of dread, Jana got out of the Jeep and was immediately buffeted by a stiff breeze. She held on to her straw sun hat and started toward the white pop-up canopy she had been told indicated the archaeologists' base of operations, dodging to avoid an honest-to-goodness tumbleweed and muttering a prayer that there be no snakes lurking behind the clumps of sagebrush she skirted.

A tall, graying man with a deeply pockmarked face looked up from a clipboard as she approached, his mouth turned down in a frown. She recognized Jeremy Eddleston, Jenny's supervisor. "I'm Jana Lassiter," she said, before he could order her away. "We met briefly at my sister's orientation."

His face relaxed, and he set the clipboard on the folding table in front of him and walked out to meet her, extending both hands. "Ms. Lassiter, it's good to see you again, though not under these circumstances. I'm so sorry for your loss."

She froze at his words, anger warring with panic in her chest. She opted for anger. "Is there some news I don't know about?" she asked. "Is my sister dead?" She had to force out the last word.

Eddleston's face turned the color of the iron-infused sandstone around them. "Of course not. I mean, we don't know... I only meant…"

She decided to let him off the hook. "It's always difficult to know what to say in a situation like this," she said.

The stiffness went out of him, his shoulders slumping so that he appeared several inches shorter. "Exactly. We're all so terribly worried about Jenny. She was such a valuable part of our team, and so well liked. We can't imagine what happened to her."

"What did happen to her?" Jana asked. "That's what I came from Denver to find out."

"We don't know." Eddleston turned and gestured toward the mesa that rose up a quarter mile or so away, its slopes heavily pocked with large boulders and clumps of scrub oak and juniper. "We've been excavating in this area all summer. Jenny, as you probably know, joined us at the beginning of June. She was helping to sift through some of the material we had recently extracted and after lunch said she was going to take a short break to stretch her legs. Her friends thought that meant she was going to use the portajohn." He indicated the bright blue portable toilet under a tree to Jana's left. "Everyone was so engrossed in the work no one noticed she hadn't returned until the team began packing up for the day a couple of hours later. They called and looked everywhere, but she didn't answer and no one could find a trace of her."

"Why didn't you call the police right away?"

Jana asked. "I understand they didn't get out here until this morning."

"There's no phone service out here," Eddleston said. "It's a ten-mile drive over rough roads to get a signal. By the time anyone realized Jenny was missing, it was getting dark. As you might imagine, this place is almost impossible to find at night. There's only the Jeep trail we've made and no lights at all."

Jana shivered, trying not to imagine Jenny out here in that darkness, hurt and alone. But the images of her sister in danger rushed in anyway.

"I was away at a meeting I had to attend," Eddleston said. "But the rest of the team searched until they couldn't see their hands in front of their faces while others went for help."

"It's true." A young man who had been standing nearby joined them. "We shouted for her until we were hoarse. This morning the park rangers and the county sheriff brought out a search dog. They even flew a helicopter, searching for any sign of her. But they didn't find anything."

Jana scanned the area again. "I don't understand," she said. "How could someone just… vanish? Jenny isn't some flighty, irresponsible schoolgirl. She's smart and sensible. She wouldn't simply wander off."

Eddleston was nodding his head like a bob-blehead doll. "I know. I've said the same thing myself. I wish I had answers for you, but I don't."

Jana opened her mouth to ask another question, but was silenced by the distinctive low crackling sound of a vehicle slowly making its way across the rocky track that passed for a road to the dig. She and Eddleston turned together to watch the approach of a black-and-white FJ Cruiser, light bar on top. The cruiser parked beside Jana's Jeep and two men in khaki uniforms and Stetsons exited.

The passenger was closest to Jana—a broad-shouldered, sandy-haired guy who would have looked right at home on a beach with a surfboard. He was clean shaven, and dark aviator glasses hid his eyes, but she had the sense he was checking her out, so she stared boldly back at him.

The driver, a slim, dark-haired man, spoke first. "I'm Officer Reynolds and this is Officer Spencer, with the Ranger Brigade. We're looking into the disappearance of Jennifer Lassiter and wanted to interview the people who were with her the day she disappeared."

"I'm Professor Jeremy Eddleston, lead archaeologist on this dig and Jennifer's supervisor." Eddleston stepped forward and offered his hand.

"Ma'am." The blond Ranger—Officer Spencer—touched the brim of his hat. "Did you work with Jennifer, also?"

"No. I'm her sister. I drove from Denver for the same reason you're here—to talk to people and try to find out what happened."

"When was the last time you talked to your sister?" Officer Spencer asked.

"We spoke the day before yesterday. She was in good spirits, enjoying her work and excited about some finds of pottery they had made." She glanced at Eddleston. "She said she liked the people she worked with."

"So she didn't mention anything that was troubling her?" Spencer asked.

"Nothing was troubling her, I'm sure," Jana said.

"Would you say you and your sister are close?" Spencer asked.

"Yes. We shared an apartment in Denver the first part of this summer, before she started the internship."

"Do you have any other siblings?" Spencer asked. "Parents?"

"Our mother and father both passed away some years ago," she said. Her mother had succumbed to cancer while Jana was still in high school, her father killed a few years later in a car accident on an icy road. "We don't have any siblings."

"And you're sure nothing was troubling your sister?" he asked again.

"Nothing was troubling her. If it had been, she would have told me. Why are you even asking these questions?"

Spencer glanced at his partner, who was deep in conversation with Eddleston. "We need to eliminate any obvious reason for your sister to walk off the job and disappear. Unfortunately, a certain percentage of missing persons are people who have chosen to run away from their responsibilities or even commit suicide. We look for things like depression, troubled relationships or financial difficulties as possible motivations. Once we eliminate those, we consider other explanations."

"Well, you'd better start considering those other explanations now. My sister wasn't depressed, she didn't have any debt, and she got along with everybody."

Spencer removed his sunglasses, the sympathy in his blue eyes catching her off guard. "What do you think happened to Jennifer?" he asked.

"I have no idea," she said. "You're supposed to find that out."

"Yes, but you knew her best. What do you think would have motivated her to leave the group? Would she want to be alone if she had had an argument with someone? Was she the type who would investigate an odd noise, or try to help an injured animal? Would she have left camp to check out an interesting rock formation, or maybe gone in search of a better cell signal?"

She relaxed a little. "I see what you're getting at." She looked around them, at the bright, windswept landscape. "I don't think she would have gone after an animal. She likes dogs and cats, but she's a little afraid of wild animals—like I am. There's apparently no cell service out here and she had been working out here long enough to know that, so there was no point in wandering around trying to find a better signal. I suppose it's possible she might have wanted some time alone if she had had an argument with someone."

"Then let's find out if that's the case." He moved to join his partner with Eddleston. "Did Jennifer have a disagreement with any of her coworkers that day?" he asked.

"Not at all," Eddleston said. "Jenny got along great with everyone."

"We'll want to talk to her coworkers and verify that," Reynolds said.

"Of course." The archaeologist squinted past them, obviously distracted. Jana turned and saw a dusty whirlwind on the horizon that drew nearer and morphed into a late-model, sand-colored Camry racing toward them. "I was wondering when he would show up," Eddleston said.

"Who is it?" Officer Spencer asked.

"Eric Patterson," Eddleston said. "He's a reporter with the Montrose paper."

Reynolds scowled. "We don't have time to talk to reporters."

"He's not just a reporter," Eddleston said. "And you probably do want to talk to him." He turned to Jana. "You, too."

"Why is that?" Jana asked.

Eddleston looked confused. "Because he's Jenny's fiancé. Didn't she tell you?"

Chapter Two

Ryan studied Jana's reaction to Eddleston's identification of the approaching visitor—shock, confusion and then anger played across a face that had the same fair beauty as her sister, but with a maturity that lent more angularity and sophistication to her features. Her eyes held more shrewdness than the photo of the missing young woman, as if she had learned the hard way to be skeptical of the promises people made.

The Camry stopped a short distance away in a cloud of red dust, and a slight young man with thinning blond hair and a boyish face stepped out. He assessed the quartet waiting for him with a glance and nodded, as if approving this welcoming party, then strode toward them and spoke in a loud voice, as if addressing a crowd. "I heard the Rangers had been assigned to the case," he said. "Now maybe we'll get some results. No offense to the local cops, but they don't have the resources and expertise you guys do."

Before either Ethan or Ryan could reply, Eric turned to Jana and seized her hand. "You must be Jana. Jenny has told me so much about you."

Jana pulled her hand away and didn't return Eric's smile. "Funny. She never mentioned you."

The wattage of his grin didn't lower. "We wanted to give you the news in person," he said. "We planned a trip to Denver to see you later this month. Jenny wanted it to be a surprise."

"So it's true—you're engaged?" Jana asked.

"Yes." He held up a hand like a cop halting traffic. "Now I know what you're thinking—Jenny is young and we haven't known each other that long—but when it's true love, I guess you just know."

"How long have you and Jenny known each other?" Ryan asked.

"Two months. We met when I was working on a story on this archaeological dig."

"Eric did a wonderful piece about our work that was picked up for the *Denver Post*,"

Eddleston said. "It was great publicity for our department."

"How long have you been engaged?" Ryan asked.

"Not long," Eric said. "We decided a couple of weeks ago, actually."

"It isn't like Jenny to keep something like this a secret from me," Jana said.

"Well, she isn't a little girl anymore, telling big sis everything," Eric said. "She wanted her own life."

Ryan felt Jana stiffen beside him. He didn't blame her. Patterson had all the subtlety of a steamroller. But an argument between the two of them wasn't going to help find Jenny. "When was the last time you spoke to Jenny?" he asked Patterson.

"We talked over breakfast at my place yesterday morning before she left to head out here for work." The way he said it—emphasizing the word *breakfast* and watching for Jana's reaction—made Ryan think he was bragging. He and Jenny had spent the night together and Patterson wanted to make sure Jana knew it. He was letting her know that he had been closer to her sister than she was.

Patterson turned to Eddleston. "I just came out to let you know I want to do anything I can to help," he said. "If you think more publicity in the paper would be useful, I'm your man."

"We'll certainly have questions for you," Ryan said before Eddleston could answer. "And we have a copy of the interview you gave the sheriff's office. Right now, we'd like to talk to some of the other people Jenny worked with."

"Of course." Eddleston gestured toward the base of the mesa, where half-a-dozen people milled about amid a grid of pink plastic flags. "Talk to anyone you like."

Ryan nodded to Jana and touched the brim of his hat. "Ma'am," he said, then followed Ethan across the rough ground toward the excavation.

When they were far enough away from the others that they couldn't be overheard, Ethan said, "Give me your impressions."

"The sister doesn't know as much about Jenny as she thought she did," Ryan said. "Eddleston is most concerned about making a good impression. The fiancé is too cocky and sure of himself and for some reason he's going out of his way to goad Jana."

"If Jenny was the only woman missing, I'd put him at the top of the suspect list," Ethan said. "But his name hasn't come up in our investigation of the first missing woman, Lucia

Raton, and it seems unlikely he knew an illegal immigrant from Guatemala who just happened to be passing through."

"So he's a jerk but probably not a killer," Ryan said.

"Provided the women are dead," Ethan said.

"Right. We don't have any bodies, but we both know the stats." When young women went missing for no reason, too often they were eventually found dead.

"Maybe this case will be an exception to the norm," Ethan said.

For the next hour, the two Rangers questioned Jenny's coworkers, who all professed sadness and shock at her disappearance. They were able to establish a timeline for yesterday. No one had noticed anything unusual before she vanished. They all agreed she hadn't seemed depressed or afraid or anything like that. "Jenny was one of these really upbeat, look-on-the-bright-side kind of people," said a twenty-year-old archaeology major, Heidi. "I used to tease her about it sometimes. If she had a flat tire on the way in, she wouldn't complain about the tire, she'd talk about how amazing it was to be in such a beautiful setting with nothing to do but wait for something to come along and help."

"So even if something had happened that

might upset most people, she wouldn't necessarily show any distress," Ethan said.

"I guess you could put it that way," Heidi said.

"What about her relationship with Eric Patterson?" Ryan asked.

Heidi slanted him a wary look. "What about it?"

"Was she happy? Excited about being engaged?"

"She never actually said anything about being engaged," Heidi said. "First I heard of it was after she disappeared and he came out with the local cops this morning and told everyone. He said they had agreed to keep it a secret until she had a chance to tell her sister."

"Did that strike you as odd—that she wouldn't have shared something like that?" Ryan asked.

She shrugged. "I don't know. I mean, it surprised me a little. I knew she had gone out with the guy a few times, but I didn't think it was that serious. I mean, they hadn't known each other long, but love makes people do crazy things sometimes, I guess."

"Tell me a little more about her mood yesterday," Ryan asked. "Did she mention anything at all about anything that had happened to upset her—an argument with someone, worry over finances, anything like that?"

Heidi shook her head. "Nothing like that. She was maybe a little quiet. When she took a break at about one, I didn't think anything of it."

"You thought she'd gone to use the restroom," Ryan said.

"At first, but then when she didn't come back, I figured she'd taken a walk. She did that sometimes, when things were slow. She was really interested in wildflowers and plants and stuff, and she liked to photograph the scenery."

"What was your first thought when you realized she was missing?"

She shrugged. "I wondered if she'd gone too far from camp and gotten lost." She swept her hand to indicate the surrounding landscape. "It's pretty empty out here. I know I get disoriented all the time. But we spread out and searched and none of us saw any sign of her. I wouldn't think she could have gone that far."

The rest of the students who had worked with Jenny shared Heidi's puzzlement as to what might have happened to Jenny. Ethan and Ryan finished their questions and headed back to the cruiser. Eric's Camry was gone and Eddleston had returned to his work, but

Ryan was surprised to find Jana Lassiter waiting beside the cruiser.

"Could I speak with you a moment?" she asked as he approached. She glanced toward Ethan. "Privately?"

"I'll start filling out the reports," Ethan said, opening the driver's-side door.

Ryan walked with Jana about fifty yards, to the shade of a pile of boulders. "What's on your mind?" he asked.

"What do you know about Eric Patterson?" she asked.

"No more than you do," he said. "I've only been in town a week. I transferred to the Rangers from Grand Junction."

She hugged her arms around her stomach, as if she was in pain. "I didn't know about him—not just that he and Jenny were engaged, but I didn't even know he existed. That isn't like Jenny. Not that I expect her to tell me everything, but she always talks to me about the men in her life."

"Maybe she didn't say anything to you about Eric because this relationship was different from those others," he said. "More serious. Maybe she wanted to be more sure of her feelings before she shared them with you."

Jana shook her head. "That isn't her. And he's not her type at all. The men she dates are always funny and easygoing. Considerate. He's so cocky and full of himself. He isn't worried about her—he's basking in the attention her disappearance is bringing to him."

Ryan couldn't disagree with anything about her assessment of Eric Patterson. "People react differently to grief," he said. "Maybe he came off cocky just now because he was nervous about meeting you and trying to impress you."

She gave him a sharp look. "Do you always feel the need to play devil's advocate?"

"It's a cop thing. Questioning assumptions is sometimes a good way to find out new information."

She sighed and her shoulders slumped. "I suppose being disagreeable doesn't mean he had anything to do with Jenny's disappearance."

"We don't have a good enough picture of what happened to have any suspects yet," Ryan said. "We have more people to interview."

"Who?"

He didn't see any harm in telling her. "There's a group camped not far from here. We want to find out if any of them saw or heard anything."

"I don't understand why you don't have more people out searching for her," Jana said. "What about using dogs to track her? And what about her phone? Can't you find someone through their cell phone? Have you issued one of those alerts—an Amber Alert? Isn't that for missing persons?" With each new suggestion, she grew more agitated.

Ryan laid a gentling hand on her shoulder. "There are search and rescue teams combing the area right now," he said. "The sheriff's office has had a tracking dog out here and we've got people trying to trace her phone, but they're not getting any kind of signal. And Amber Alerts are only for children. Your sister hasn't been missing even twenty-four hours. There's still a chance she'll turn up unharmed. Maybe she just needed to get away for a while. She could have hitched a ride into town and be staying with a friend we don't know about."

She stared into his eyes, as if trying to read his thoughts and divine his intentions. "She wouldn't let me worry this way," she said. "If Jenny was with a friend, or anywhere she could make a call, she would let me know she was all right. I've tried calling and texting her dozens of times, but she isn't answering her phone. I'm really worried about her."

He took his hand from her shoulder and nodded. "From what you've told me, it does seem unusual for your sister to just walk away from everything. Right now, our best guess is that she is lost, so we'll continue the search efforts, including interviewing everyone who might have seen her."

She opened her purse and took out a business card. She scribbled something on the back, then handed it to him. "That's my cell number. I'm staying at the Columbine Inn. If you learn anything new, please call me."

He glanced at the number, then turned the card over. "You're a CPA?"

"You sound surprised."

His face felt hot. "It wouldn't have been my first guess."

"I get it. CPAs are supposed to be boring and plain. I hear librarians have the same problem."

"You aren't boring or plain." He slipped the card into his pocket. "I promise to keep in touch."

"I'm trusting you to do that." She met his gaze and he felt the pull of that look somewhere deep in his gut—a surprising but not wholly unpleasant sensation. "And just so you know, I don't give my trust very easily," she added, before turning and walking away.

JANA'S FIRST INSTINCT was to remain near the dig site, walking the desert and calling for her sister. But she had no idea where Jenny might go, and in the vast, mostly featureless terrain she was liable to end up lost herself. So she returned to Montrose, but not to the motel. Instead, she headed to the apartment Jenny shared with another young woman. April was a medical assistant at the local hospital, and she had told Jana to feel free to come in and look around.

She let herself in with the key Jenny had given her and stood for a moment surveying the living room. She had been here before, of course, on visits since Jenny had relocated here for the summer. But she had never been here without Jenny. Already the place felt alien without her sister's presence.

Steeling herself, she crossed the living room to Jenny's bedroom. She didn't know what she was looking for—what she might find that the police investigators wouldn't have uncovered. April had told her the police had already been there. They had made copies of Jenny's computer files and looked through her belongings, but shared no impressions of their findings.

Jana sat on the side of the bed and looked around, trying to see the room as an outsider might. The small space was as bright and sunny as Jenny herself—from the pink patchwork quilt on the bed to the paper flowers tacked to the bulletin board over her desk. Sophisticated cosmetics shared space with a stuffed pink bear. It was the room of a girl who was slowly transforming into a woman.

She swallowed hard against the lump in her throat. She refused to give in to tears, as if grieving would be disloyal. But the knowledge that her sister might not be all right, might in fact be dead, lurked at the edge of her consciousness, a horrible specter she wasn't yet willing to confront.

It's only been one day, she reminded herself. Jenny is young and healthy and smart. If she did get lost, she knows to stay put and wait for help. And she's got a lot of people working to find her. The memory of Officer Spencer's hand on her shoulder, a reassuring, comforting weight, returned and made her feel more settled. She believed he was doing everything he could to help her and Jenny. In the future, the sisters would look back on this time and laugh about the adventure.

She forced herself to stand and walk to the desk and power up the laptop computer. She knew the password—the same one Jenny had used for years—and soon was perusing her sister's files and email and Facebook page. Nothing seemed out of the ordinary. There was no journal detailing a secret worry or hurt, no anguished emails to friends, only the usual cheery greetings or gossiping about school or movies or weekend plans. She found a few emails from Eric Patterson, but they offered little insight into the relationship—invitations to dinner or confirmation of weekend plans. No words of love or secret scheming.

The sound of the front door opening startled her. "April, is that you?" she called. "I'm back here in Jenny's room."

"It's not April," came a man's voice, and a moment later Officer Ryan Spencer filled the doorway of the bedroom.

Heart thudding painfully, Jana stared at him, caught off guard. "What are you doing here?" she demanded.

"The sheriff's office gave us the information they had, but I wanted to see the place for myself." He came into the room, and the already-small space seemed to shrink around them. "I thought it would help me get a better feel for your sister."

Jana sank onto the bed again, fearful her shaking legs might not support her. Having the police here—in Jenny's private space—made the magnitude of her disappearance that much greater. "This room is just like Jenny," she said. She didn't elaborate—let him make of that what he would.

His gaze roamed around the room. She had the sense that he was analyzing everything he saw, putting each item into a bigger picture he was forming of her sister. At last his eyes came back to her. "Have you found anything I should know about?" he asked.

She glanced toward the desk and the open computer. "I don't know if it's anything important," she said. "But it's something that struck me as odd when I was looking through her social media."

"There are no pictures online of her with Eric Patterson," he said.

"Yes!" She stared at him, impressed in spite of herself. "She has pictures of herself with other friends on her Facebook and Instagram pages, and here." She indicated the bulletin board.

He nodded. "If you were engaged to someone, you would probably have lots of pictures of them." He walked over to the laptop and hit a few keys. "There's something else on this you ought to see," he said. "Something I discovered looking at the copy of her hard drive the sheriff's office made."

"They made a copy of her hard drive?" She didn't know whether to be comforted by their thoroughness or alarmed that the investigation was moving so quickly.

"We've learned the hard way that we need to take these cases seriously from the start," he said. "There was a time when adults had to be missing for a while before law enforcement stepped in, but now we know the sooner we launch an investigation, the more likely we are to have a positive outcome."

She nodded. "That makes sense. So what did you find?"

"Come look."

Feeling steadier now, she stood and came to stand beside him, studying the screen, which showed a handsome, dark-haired man dressed in white, next to a blog post about the key to happiness. "What am I looking at?" she asked.

"It's a blog by a man named Daniel Metwater. He calls himself a prophet and preaches a kind of back-to-nature spirituality a lot of young people find very compelling. Jenny's browser history shows she had read quite a few of his posts and bookmarked his site."

"Why is that important?" Jana asked.

"Because Metwater and his followers are camped very near where Jenny disappeared."

Her stomach gave a nervous jump. "You mentioned wanting to question some people who were camped nearby. Did you mean this man, Metwater?"

"Yes, but I haven't talked to him yet."

"Why not?"

"I wanted to see what I could find out here first."

"I want to go with you when you talk to him," she said.

"No." The word held all the finality of a slamming door, but she intended to push that door open.

"I can help you," she said. "People will say things to me they won't say to a cop."

He shook his head, his jaw tense, blue eyes boring into her with an intensity that any other time would have been intimidating. But she had too much at stake to back down now. "If you don't take me with you, I'll go out there on my own," she said.

"I can't have you interfering with my case," he said.

"This may be your case, but she's my sister." She hated the tremor in her voice as she said the last words and fought hard to control it. "I will do everything in my power to find her. I'll talk to anyone and everyone who might have information that can help me find her, and you can't stop me."

"I could have you arrested for interfering with an investigation."

"You could. But would you really do that?

When we met earlier today, you didn't strike me as a jerk."

He actually flinched at the word, as if she had slapped him. "Am I supposed to take that as a compliment?"

"Take it however you like." She lifted her chin and met his gaze, ignoring the tremor in her stomach as he leaned closer. She could smell the leather-and-starch scent of him, masculine and clean, and see the muscle jump along his jaw as he considered his answer.

"If I let you come with me, you can't take part in questioning Metwater," he said. "That has to be done by the book if we're going to get anything we might be able to use in court later."

"I understand. I thought I could mix with his followers. Find out if any of them know Jenny, or if she's been in the camp."

He rubbed his jaw, the scrape of beard against his palm sending another shiver of awareness through her. "You could talk to some of the women in the group," he said. "I don't expect them to be very cooperative with the police—they haven't made any secret of their dislike of law enforcement. But they might be more sympathetic to you."

She fought the impulse to throw her arms around him and kiss him—not so much because she thought he might object, but because she didn't trust herself to stop with one friendly kiss. This sexy cop got to her in a way that alarmed her. The last thing she needed now was that kind of distraction. "I won't get in your way," she said. "But we could work together."

His expression hardened again. "No offense, but I don't need your help. My job is to solve this case and find your sister."

She opened her mouth to argue, then thought better of it. He had agreed to what she wanted, so she might as well stay in his good graces—for now. "Do you think this man—Metwater—had something to do with Jenny's disappearance?" she asked.

"We don't know," Ryan said. "Right now, let's just say he's a person of interest."

"That means he's a suspect," she said, her heart beating faster again.

"I didn't say that. If you come with me, you can't do anything to interfere with the investigation and you can't share anything we see or do with reporters. Especially not with Eric Patterson."

She made a face. "I don't have any desire to talk to him. Maybe it's petty, but he rubs me the wrong way."

He nodded, as if he agreed with her. "When

you meet Metwater, maybe you can tell us if he's someone who would have interested Jenny—would she have followed him into the wilderness?"

She swallowed past the sudden tightness in her throat. "And the more important question—if she did, why didn't she come back?"

Chapter Three

Daniel Metwater and his followers had set up camp in a shady grove near a freshwater spring at the base of Mystic Mesa. Ryan parked his cruiser next to a dilapidated pickup, and Ethan slid his vehicle in next to Ryan's. "I don't see anything," Jana said, climbing out of Ryan's vehicle and looking around. Though the sun was slipping toward the horizon, casting long shadows from the trees and boulders, there was still plenty of daylight left this time of year.

"It's up in the trees through here." Ethan pointed to a narrow path into the underbrush. He led the way, with Jana following and Ryan bringing up the rear.

They had only walked about ten yards when a shirtless man with blond dreadlocks stepped out in front of them. He carried a heavy wooden staff, which would have made

an effective weapon. He took in the two uni-
formed officers and scarcely glanced at Jana,
then settled on Ethan. "Is there a problem, Officer?" he asked.

"We have some questions for Mr. Metwater," Ethan said, and started to move past him.

Blondie stepped in front of them, holding
the stick across his body. "I'm not supposed
to let anyone into camp without permission?"
His voice rose in a question at the end of the
sentence and he looked doubtful.

"This badge means we don't need permission." Ethan stepped toward him again.
Blondie glanced at Ryan, then moved off the
path. The two officers and Jana filed by and
entered a clearing around which were clus-
tered a ragtag collection of tents, trailers and
makeshift shacks. A dozen or more adults,
most of them young women, and half-a-dozen
small children milled around the area.

A tall man with a sharp, intelligent face
looked up from a conversation with an at-
tractive pregnant woman. Dark curls framed
classically handsome features, but a scowl
wrinkled his brow, and at the sight of the newcomers, everyone around him and the woman
shrank away. "Hello, Mr. Metwater." Ethan
addressed him. "Ms. Mattheson."

"Asteria, you may wait for me in the motor

home," Metwater said. Ryan realized the blonde must be Andi Mattheson. According to the information Simon had given him, she was the daughter of a former senator and perhaps Daniel Metwater's most famous disciple. Without a second glance at the visitors, she slipped away.

"I thought we had reached an understanding that the Rangers were not to harass me and my family anymore," Metwater said. "Or did my attorneys not make that clear enough?"

Ryan pulled out his phone, woke it to display the photo of Jennifer Lassiter and turned the screen toward Metwater. "Have you seen this woman?" he asked.

Metwater peered at the image and shook his head. "No. Who is she?"

"How about this one?" Ryan scrolled to a photo of Alicia Mendoza.

"No." Metwater folder his arms over his muscular chest. "What is this about?"

"Do the names Jennifer Lassiter or Alicia Mendoza mean anything to you?"

Instead of answering, Metwater turned to Jana. "Who are you?" he asked. "You don't look like a cop."

"I'm Jana Lassiter," she said, pale but composed. "Jennifer Lassiter is my sister. She disappeared yesterday, from the archaeological dig near here."

Metwater turned back to the officers. "So of course you think I had something to do with this woman's disappearance, even though I've never met her or even heard of her."

Before Ryan or Ethan could speak, Jana stepped between them and Metwater. "Jenny had your blog bookmarked on her computer," she said. "She had been reading it right before she disappeared. We were hoping she came here to meet you."

Metwater's expression softened, and Ryan had a sense of the kind of charm that might persuade people that he had the answers they were seeking. "I'm sorry I can't help you," he said. "I never met your sister." He turned to the Rangers. "What about this other woman? Was she a fan of mine, also? I have many people who are interested in the message I have to share, but my aim is to help, not harm."

"Alicia Mendoza also disappeared very near here," Ethan said. "She was traveling through the area with a group of illegal immigrants. It's possible she became lost and sought refuge in your camp."

"Many things are possible," Metwater said. "But she never came here."

"What about Easy? Has he been around lately?" Ethan asked.

Ryan had to think a moment to remember who Ethan was referring to. Some notes from an earlier interview with the women in Metwater's camp had mentioned someone named Easy who had been seen with Lucia Raton when she left the Family's camp.

"I haven't seen him, no," Metwater said. "He's not a member of the Family."

"But he hangs out here sometimes, we understand," Ethan said.

"I don't require visitors to sign in and out."

"So it's possible Alicia Mendoza or Jennifer Lassiter were here and you didn't know about it," Ryan said.

"It's possible," Metwater said. "But not probable." He glared at them, defiant.

"If you hear anything about either woman— or about Easy—please let us know," Ethan said.

"We avoid mixing with the outside world as much as possible," Metwater said.

"Yet you welcome new members." Ryan looked around the camp—there didn't seem to be a shortage of people who wanted to join Metwater's group, despite the primitive living conditions.

"People come to me seeking a retreat from

the false atmosphere of so-called civilized life," Metwater said.

Ryan eyed the motor home parked at the far edge of the clearing. The gleaming RV sported a solar array on the roof and was large enough to comfortably accommodate several people. While some of the Prophet's followers were roughing it, the man himself lived in wilderness luxury.

Metwater noticed the direction of Ryan's gaze. "I left a life of privilege to find a better way," he said. "The fact that my message resonates with so many people should tell you I preach the truth."

Plenty of charlatans and con artists managed to charm untold number of hapless victims. Until Ryan saw evidence to the contrary, he would assume Metwater fell into that camp.

"Mr. Metwater does speak the truth, at least about his background."

Ryan turned toward the new voice that had addressed them. "Hello officers, Jana," Eric Patterson said. "I was wondering when you would get around to showing up here."

"WHAT ARE YOU doing here?" Jana stared at the reporter. Had he decided to investigate Jenny's disappearance on his own? Or was her sister's supposed fiancé a member of Metwater's group?

"I invited him," Daniel Metwater said. "Eric is my special guest."

Eric's smile echoed Metwater's own. Jana thought they looked like two politicians posing for a photo op, their grins too large and not quite reaching their eyes. "I'm writing a profile of the Prophet for my paper," the reporter said. "We're privileged to have a figure of such national interest living in our area."

Jana glanced at Metwater. Was he really of national interest? She had certainly never heard of him, but then, she wasn't searching for meaning in her life or lost with nowhere to go, or any of the other things Ryan had said attracted people to this remote camp. And neither was Jenny.

Maybe one of Jenny's friends had told her about Metwater, and she had been reading his blog out of curiosity. Jenny was always interested in new things, but that didn't mean she had decided to follow this false prophet into the wilderness.

"I thought you avoided mixing with the outside world," Ryan said. "Or don't newspapers count?"

"It's another way to spread his message," Eric said before Metwater could answer.

"I guess it's another way to solicit financial contributions, too." Ryan's eyes met Jana's, as if they shared an inside joke, and a jolt of pleasure shot through her. She did feel as if she and this cop were allies, that she wasn't alone in her longing to have Jenny returned to her safely.

"Cynics like you scoff, but I could tell you a dozen stories of people whose lives have been changed by my message," Metwater said.

"And I want to hear all of them," Eric said.

"Mr. Patterson," Jana began.

"Please, call me Eric," he said. "After all, we're practically related."

Jana clenched her teeth to keep from telling him they were definitely not related. She couldn't understand what Jenny saw in this man, but until her sister could confide in her, better to hold her tongue. "Did you know Jenny followed Mr. Metwater's blog?" she asked.

"Of course," he said. "Her interest in the Prophet led me to pitch his story to my editor." He turned to Metwater. "I'm only sorry my fiancée isn't here to meet you. She is a great admirer of yours."

"The loss is mine," Metwater said.

"You're sure Jenny never came here on her own or with you?" Ethan asked.

"I'm positive," Eric said. "We planned to come here together."

"Maybe she got curious, and knowing Metwater and his followers were camped so close, she decided to check things out on her own," Ryan said.

"I already told you, she hasn't been here," Metwater said.

"You told us the same thing about Lucia Raton," Ethan said. "Then we found out later she had been to see you."

Metwater pressed his lips together, but said nothing more.

"Jenny wouldn't have come here without me," Eric said. "We had planned to go together and she wouldn't dishonor those plans."

"What does honor have to do with it?" Jana asked, unable to contain her exasperation. "If Jenny wanted to do something, she did it. She didn't need your permission."

"Since you don't live here and aren't a part of Jenny's everyday life, you don't understand how close the two of us are," Eric said. "She wanted to share new experiences with me. When you truly love someone, doing things without them isn't as satisfying."

His patronizing tone set her teeth on edge. "Since when does getting engaged to someone mean you're joined at the hip?" she muttered.

"Now that we've established that you're wasting your time questioning me or my followers, I have an interview to conduct." Metwater put a hand on Eric's shoulder.

"We haven't established anything," Ryan said. But Metwater and Eric had already turned away.

Ryan started toward the pair, but Ethan stopped him. "We'll get back to those two later. In the meantime, let's talk to a few of the faithful." He nodded to Jana. "Mingle with the women and see what you can find out. Even if these people didn't have anything to do with your sister's disappearance, they might have seen or heard something."

"All right."

The two officers moved away, leaving her standing by herself. She tried to ignore the nervous flutter in her stomach and headed toward a group of women who stood in front of a large white tent near the motor home. At her approach, they all turned as if to retreat into the tent. "Please, don't leave," she called out. "I'm not a police officer. I just want to talk to you."

"You're with the police." A severe-looking woman with curly brown hair addressed her in a scolding tone. "You want to hassle us, the way they always do."

"I don't want to hassle anyone," Jana said.

"I'm only trying to find my sister." She turned her phone toward them to show a recent photograph she had taken of Jenny, who was smiling broadly and looked so young and happy and alive. It didn't seem real that she could have simply vanished.

"We don't know her," the pregnant blonde who had been with Metwater when Jana and the others had arrived in camp said, not unkindly. "We can't help you."

"The archaeological dig where she worked is very close to here," Jana said. "Did you know anyone else from there?"

The women exchanged glances. "We didn't know anyone," the oldest of the trio, with white-blond hair and pale eyes said.

"But you know something about them you're not telling me," Jana said. She hadn't missed the significance of the look between them.

"We visited them a few times," the pretty blonde said. "They showed us some of the pottery shards and other artifacts they found."

"Who showed you?" Jana asked.

"Not your sister," the brown-haired woman said. "We never talked to her."

Jana slumped, trying to hide her disappointment.

"We saw her, though," the older woman said. "She was with that reporter."

"Eric?" Jana asked.

"Yeah. That one." The brown-haired woman's sour expression left little doubt of her opinion of Eric Patterson. "They were arguing. Pretty loudly, too."

"What were they arguing about?" Jana asked.

The pretty blonde shook her head. "We couldn't tell, but she was pretty upset. At one point she shoved him."

"What did he do?" Jana asked.

"Nothing," the blonde said. "He was pretty calm about the whole thing, but she was really worked up."

"Did you overhear anything at all?" Jana asked. "Could you guess what she was upset about?"

All three women shook their heads. "They were standing too far away," the older woman said.

"I saw her one other time," the brown-haired woman said. "I went by myself a few weeks ago to try to sell some stuff I had found to the head guy."

"What kind of stuff?" Jana asked.

"Some arrowheads and spear points, but he said the items I had weren't worth anything. A woman who looked a lot like the picture you showed us was with him when I got there. They looked pretty friendly." She smirked.

"What do you mean, 'friendly'?" Jana asked.

"They were kissing," the brown-haired woman said. "Going at it pretty hot and heavy, too," she said. "When I showed up they broke it off and the girl hurried away."

"But I'm sure Professor Eddleston is married," Jana said, trying to absorb this new information.

"He was wearing a ring," the brown-haired woman said. "So maybe instead of thinking the Prophet had anything to do with your sister's disappearance, you should check out her professor's wife."

Chapter Four

Ryan and Ethan's questions to Metwater's followers turned up nothing of interest. Most people the two officers approached turned away, disappearing into tents or trailers or slipping into the surrounding trees. Others were polite but responded to all questions with bland comments about the weather. No one would admit to having seen or heard of any of the missing women, or the mysterious Easy. "We're wasting our time here," Ryan said, turning away from an affable redhead who, when asked about the missing women, commented on the mild temperatures for this time of year.

"Metwater probably coached them on what to say to us," Ethan said. "Non-confrontational, but also completely unhelpful."

"I'd almost prefer confrontation." Ryan looked around and spotted Jana with a trio of women across the camp. As he and Ethan approached, the women hurried away. "Are you ready to leave?" he asked.

"Yes." Not waiting for a response, she turned and walked ahead of them to the parking area. She was standing by Ryan's cruiser when he arrived, and said nothing as they climbed into the vehicle and drove away.

"Something bugging you?" he asked, after another long minute of silence.

"Hmm?" She glanced at him, worry lines creasing her forehead.

"You're being awfully quiet. I thought maybe you were upset about something."

She looked away again, gaze fixed on the horizon. Ryan focused on the rough road, giving her time. He hoped she would trust him enough to share what was on her mind, whether it related to the case or not. "If you had asked me two days ago if I was close to my sister, I would have said yes. We were as close as two people could be," she said after a moment. "But now I feel like I was just lying to myself. I don't know Jenny at all. I'm asking people questions about her that I think I know the answers to, and the person they're describing to me is a stranger."

"Maybe it's not that you didn't know your

sister, but that other people see her differently," he said.

"I didn't know about her engagement to Eric Patterson." She half turned to face him once more. "And just now, one of Daniel Metwater's followers told me she saw Jenny kissing Jeremy Eddleston."

That was a twist Ryan hadn't seen coming. "When did they see this? And where?"

"Last week. At the dig site. They said it was a very passionate kiss."

"Maybe they misinterpreted. Or even if they didn't, it's not that unusual for coworkers to become involved."

"Eddleston is married," Jana said. "And he's old enough to be Jenny's father. Why would she become involved with an older, married man—one of her professors?"

He tightened his grip on the steering wheel, her obvious distress making him want to reach for her—or to shake the person who had upset her so much. "From what little I've learned, your sister does strike me as smarter than that," he said. "But young people do make mistakes."

"She never said a word to me about being interested in Eddleston," she said. "But then, she wouldn't, would she? She would know I wouldn't approve." She faced forward once more, hands knotted in her lap. "Should I ask him about it? Or will I only make things worse if I confront him? Jenny would say I'm interfering—that it's none of my business."

"I'll take you back to your car, then I'll talk to him," he said.

"No. I want to go with you. I want to see his face when you confront him with this."

He stifled a groan. Did they have to go through this again? "I can't have you there when I question a potential suspect," he said.

"Why not?" she asked. "He's more likely to let down his guard with me there, don't you think? And I've already proved I can be useful to you, haven't I?"

"You're not an unbiased witness," he said.

"Are you? Aren't the police supposed to be on the side of the victim?"

"That's not the same as being related to her. You can't come with me."

"Fine. Then pull over."

"What?"

"Pull the car over. Now." She took hold of the door handle.

"What do you think you're doing?" he asked, alarmed.

"I'll walk from here to the dig site. I'll talk to Eddleston on my own and someone there can give me a ride back to my car."

"Don't test me," he said.

"And don't give me that line about arresting me for interfering with your case. I have every right to talk to the people who know my sister. If it was your sister wouldn't you do the same?"

Her stubbornness made him want to pull out his hair—but at the same time he admired her loyalty and determination to do everything in her power to find her sister. And she had proved she had a steady head on her shoulders and that people would talk to her. He eased the cruiser to the side of the road. "Don't get out," he said. "I'll take you with me. If I don't, you're liable to get us both in more trouble."

"I admire a man who can admit he was wrong," she said.

He made a growling noise in the back of his throat and headed the cruiser back in the direction they had come.

"If Eddleston and Jenny were involved, maybe he knows more than he's letting on about her disappearance," she said.

"Or maybe he was responsible," Ryan said. "Either directly or indirectly. Maybe they had a fight and she wandered off to calm down and got lost."

"The women I spoke with at Metwater's camp thought Eddleston's wife might have found out about the affair and done something to Jenny," Jana said.

"Why do they think that?"

"I don't know." She had been too stunned by the bombshell they had dropped to question them about it. "But it makes sense, doesn't it? A woman whose husband is cheating on her would be understandably angry with the other woman."

"Do you know his wife?"

"No. I don't even know Eddleston, really. I met him when Jenny started the internship. I assumed he's married because he wears a wedding ring." She hugged her arms across her chest. "But maybe that's what I get for making assumptions."

He keyed in his police radio. "Ethan, do you read me?"

"What's up?" Ethan's voice crackled over the radio. "I thought I lost you."

"I'm headed back to the archaeological dig. I have a few questions I need to ask Eddleston."

"Do you need backup?"

"No, thanks. I'll fill you in when I get back to headquarters."

"Ten-four."

"Will you question Eddleston's wife, too?" Jana asked.

"Probably."

"And then she'll know about Jenny. And her life will be ruined, too. What was my sister thinking?"

"I wonder if Eric Patterson knew about this," Ryan said.

"How could he not?" she said. "How is it even possible to be engaged to one man and carrying on an affair with another and not have them find out about each other?" She shook her head. "Maybe it's not even true. Maybe those women didn't see what they thought they saw. That's the only explanation that makes sense." The only explanation that fit with Jana's image of her sister.

Ryan parked the cruiser in front of the empty shade canopies at the dig site. In the distance, a group of people worked at the base of the mesa. Jana shaded her eyes with her hand and peered in that direction. "I think I see Eddleston," she said.

Ryan started walking toward the dig, Jana close behind him. His boots left deep imprints in the thick dust and heat shimmered off the rocks around them. He was very aware of the woman beside him, the floral scent of her perfume faint in the air around him, the soft pant of her breath as they labored up a small incline. Professor Eddleston looked up from examining a pottery shard with a magnifying glass as they approached. "Has there been some news about Jenny?" he asked.

"Not yet," Ryan said. "But I have a few more questions for you."

"Of course." Eddleston handed the shard and the magnifying glass to a young man and wiped his hands on the front of his khaki trousers.

"Let's move back into the shade." Ryan nodded toward the shade canopies.

"All right." Eddleston walked beside them toward the canopies. "We're really feeling Jenny's absence on the project," he said. "She's a hard worker and everyone here likes her."

"So you and she get along well?" Jana asked. Ryan didn't miss the edge in her voice, but Eddleston didn't seem to notice.

"We're a very cohesive team on this dig," he said. "Jenny fits in very well with the group."

They reached the shade canopies and Eddleston sat on the edge of one of the folding tables, his posture relaxed. "What do you need to know?" he asked.

"Another person we interviewed reported seeing you and Jenny Lassiter kissing passionately," Ryan said. "I want to know what that's about."

All the color left Eddleston's face. He stared

at Ryan, mouth opened, and then the color returned, red flooding his cheeks. "Who told you that? When?"

Not a good sign that he didn't deny it. "So it's true? You were kissing her?"

"It wasn't what they thought. Jenny and I were friends. I…" He looked at Jana, who was glaring at him with open hostility.

"Were you having an affair with Jenny Lassiter?" Ryan asked.

Eddleston stared at the ground, mute.

"We're going to question the rest of the team about this," Ryan said. "Someone will know. It's impossible to keep relationships secret in a small group like this."

Eddleston made a choking sound. Ryan wondered if he was sobbing. After a long silence the professor cleared his throat. "Jenny and I went out a few times," he said. "My wife and I were separated. It was just for fun. It wasn't serious."

"Did Jenny know it wasn't serious?" Jana asked.

Eddleston glanced at her again. "Of course she did. Apparently, the whole time she was seeing me, she was also dating Eric Patterson. She was engaged to him—a fact I didn't even know until she disappeared."

"You didn't know Jenny and Eric were engaged?" Jana asked.

"I had no idea until he showed up at camp looking for her," Eddleston said. "I'd seen them together a few times, but I never dreamed there was anything serious between them. Frankly, she didn't even act as if she liked the guy that much."

"Does your wife know about the affair?" Ryan asked.

His face paled again. "No! And there's no need for her to. She and I are back together. We're trying to fix our marriage."

"Did Jenny know you and your wife were back together?" Jana asked.

"She did. And she was very cool about it. She wished me luck. That's how I know our relationship wasn't serious. We were both just having fun."

"Are you in the habit of seducing students?" Jana asked.

Eddleston drew himself up to his full height, his body rigid. "I did not seduce anyone," he said. "Jenny actually propositioned me. I'd be lying if I said I wasn't flattered, and surprised, too."

"Why were you surprised?" Ryan asked.

He grimaced. "Please, Officer, I know what I look like. I'm no movie star and Jenny is genuinely beautiful. She has no shortage of good-looking men her own age who would have been happy to date her. But she wanted to go out with me."

"Did she say why?" Ryan asked.

He let out a sigh and his shoulders slumped. "She said I made her feel safe. Not the greatest romantic declaration, but show me a man my age who isn't vulnerable to a young, beautiful woman's proposition and I'll show you a dead man or a saint."

"Safe from what?" Ryan asked. "Was she afraid of something—or someone?"

Eddleston shook his head. "I have no idea. I mean, she isn't a timid girl or anything like that."

"And you have no idea when she started seeing Eric Patterson, or when they got engaged?" Ryan asked.

"No."

Ryan studied him. So far, he had a sense Eddleston was telling the truth, but some people were better liars than others. "How did you feel when you found out?" he asked.

"I was upset." Eddleston shrugged. "While we were dating I thought we were exclusive. That's the impression I got." He turned to Jana. "Jenny didn't strike me as the kind of woman who keeps a lot of guys on a string.

She's sweet. Kind of the girl-next-door type. But then this Patterson guy tells me they're engaged and I don't know what to think."

"What did you do when you found out about the engagement?" Ryan asked.

"There wasn't anything I could do. Jenny had disappeared. I was worried about her."

"Were you still seeing Jenny at the time of her disappearance?"

"We weren't dating anymore, no. We ended it a couple of weeks ago. I told her I wanted to try to fix things with my wife." He twisted the ring on his finger.

"Jenny was okay with that?" Ryan asked.

"I already told you she was."

"So the two of you didn't argue about it or anything?"

"No!" He leaned toward Ryan. "What are you getting at?"

"Breakups are usually rough," Ryan said. "Maybe she was upset you were going back to your wife. Or maybe you found out about Eric and were angry she'd been two-timing you. You had an argument, one thing led to another..." He let the sentence hang, the atmosphere heavy with the unspoken accusation.

"We didn't argue," Eddleston said. "And I didn't know she was engaged to Eric. I'm not even sure when they became engaged. It could have happened after we split."

"He says they've been engaged a couple of weeks," Jana said.

Eddleston compressed his mouth in a tight line but gave no answer.

"What do you think led Jenny to walk off the job yesterday afternoon?" Ryan asked. "Was it because she was upset?"

"I don't know anything about that," he said. "She wasn't upset with me." He turned to Jana. "I like your sister. She's a sweet girl and we had a good time. We were friends— we are friends. Neither one of us did anything wrong."

"Someone did something wrong," Jana said. "My sister is missing and no one can tell me what happened to her."

"If I knew, I would tell you," Eddleston said. "I hope you find her soon. And that she's safe."

"I'm going to have to talk to your wife, and to the rest of the archaeological team," Ryan said.

Eddleston's head dropped, but he nodded. "Do what you have to do. I'll say again—we didn't do anything wrong."

"If that's true, you don't have anything to

worry about. But we may have more questions for you."

"I'll be here," Eddleston said. "I still have work to do, despite these unpleasant interruptions."

"Go back to work," Ryan said. "I'll be in touch."

He walked away, head bent, shoulders slumped. Ryan tried to figure what pretty young Jenny Lassiter had seen in the man. Jana walked over to stand beside him. "Do you think he's telling the truth?" she asked.

"Do you? Do you think Jenny would have propositioned him?"

The pain in her eyes made him ache for her. "I don't know. On one hand, Jenny always did have unconventional tastes in men."

"What do you mean, unconventional?"

"She didn't necessarily go for the classically handsome jocks. In high school, she dated geeks and outsider types. She liked artists and musicians and nerds. Looks really didn't seem to matter at all to her."

"What about her telling him he made her feel safe?"

Jana shook her head. "I don't know. She never mentioned being afraid of anything to me, and she wasn't a timid woman. She likes new people and adventures."

"And she never said anything to you about Eddleston or Patterson. Did she usually tell you about the men she dated?"

"Not every one of them, I'm sure, but certainly anyone she was serious about."

"According to Eddleston, that excludes him."

"Yes, and she might not have said anything about him because she knew I wouldn't approve."

"Because he was older?"

"Yes, and because he's married. I'm not a prude, but I draw the line at some things. I thought Jenny felt the same, but I guess not."

Impulsively, he reached out and squeezed her shoulder. "Don't beat yourself up over this," he said. "If your sister was keeping secrets from you, it was probably because she felt guilty or was afraid of disappointing you—not because she was trying to shut you out of her life."

"Thanks for saying that, even if I don't really believe it."

"Do you want to come with me while I talk to the others?"

She shook her head. "I've heard about all I can stand today. I need time to process it all."

"I need to speak to everyone now," he said.

"Before Eddleston has time to influence what they might say."

"I understand. I'll wait for you in the cruiser."

Not pausing for a response, she began walking toward the vehicle. He'd noticed that when she made a decision, she acted on it without waiting for input from others. He couldn't decide if that was a sign of someone who was impulsive or a person who was confident in her own abilities.

She had warned him she didn't trust easily, but he found himself wanting more and more to earn that trust—to prove that she could be confident in his abilities as well.

JANA WAITED IN the passenger seat of the cruiser, a hot breeze bringing in the scents of dusty juniper and the almost musical ring of tools on rock carried from the dig site at the foot of the mesa. Despite the presence of the archaeological crew, the landscape looked empty—not a building or a fence or even a power line in sight. Jenny had raved about how beautiful the country was and how much she was enjoying exploring it with friends.

Was she out there in that vastness now, lost in a remote box canyon, or lying injured at the bottom of a ravine? Jana pushed the disturbing images away and picked up her phone.

She scrolled through her photos, many of her and Jenny together. Here they were at a restaurant in Denver, toasting the camera with twin glasses of iced tea. Here was a shot of Jenny in pajamas, her feet up on the balcony railing at Jana's apartment, sticking her tongue out at Jana because she hadn't wanted her picture taken.

She stopped on a photo of the two sisters mugging for a selfie taken not far from here—at one of the scenic overlooks in Black Canyon of the Gunnison National Park. Jenny had just landed the summer internship and Jana had come out for the weekend to help her celebrate. They had attended the welcome orientation where Jana had met Professor Eddleston, toured the national park, eaten at Jenny's favorite Mexican restaurant and spent the weekend doing what they did best—hanging out and enjoying each other's company.

Jana's eyes burned. She blinked rapidly and hurriedly scrolled to her text messages. Had there been anything there to indicate that Jenny was upset or worried—or in love with a man Jana hadn't even met? She scrolled back to the messages the sisters had exchanged since Jana's weekend visit.

First day was long and harder than I thought
but so much fun. I am going to love this!

Jana read through the almost daily texts.
The very ordinariness of the exchanges made
her smile. Jenny got sunburned. She bought a
straw hat. She ate at an amazing pho restaurant. She bought a new dress, went out with
friends, flirted with a cute guy at the car wash.
She was doing work she loved, having fun
with friends—everything a nineteen-year-old
could want.

No mention of any dates. That hadn't surprised Jana. The two sisters had each had long
periods when they didn't date. They were too
busy with work and friends to have time for
one-on-one relationships with men. Yet, apparently, for most of this time period, Jenny
had been dating Jeremy Eddleston and/or Eric
Patterson.

Why had she kept these men a secret from
Jana, when Jenny was so open about everything else in her life? Jana read through the
rest of the messages, up until two days before—the last day she had heard from Jenny.
She had practically memorized these last com-
munications: Jenny was thinking about coming to Denver for Labor Day weekend. She
needed to have the oil changed in her car. She

wanted to take some more advanced archaeology classes this fall. She hoped she could get a part-time job waiting tables that wouldn't interfere with her class schedule.

Jana stilled, her finger poised over the screen, and stared at the last text from Jenny. One she knew she hadn't seen before.

Jana, I'm scared. I think I've made a big mistake and gone and gotten myself in big trouble.

Chapter Five

Several members of the archaeological crew had indicated that Heidi was closest to Jenny, so Ryan sought her out again. He found her kneeling beside a pile of rocks, carefully sorting through the fist-sized to head-sized chunks, separating them into piles. When his shadow fell over her, she looked up. "Hello, Officer." Her smile was warm. She tucked a lock of long blond hair behind one ear. "Nice to see you again."

He didn't have time to waste flirting with her. "Why didn't you tell me Jenny was involved with Professor Eddleston?" he asked.

She flushed a deep pink and sat back on her heels. "What…what are you talking about?" she stammered.

"You can't help Jenny by lying." He held out his hand. She took it and he pulled her to her feet. "Eddleston told me himself that he and Jenny dated. Why didn't you tell me?"

She bit her lower lip, a gesture that made her look even younger. "I didn't think it was important," she said. "I mean, she told me they had decided not to date anymore. He was going back to his wife and she was seeing Eric. So it was old news." She shrugged.

"Was the split amicable?"

"I guess. I mean, they seemed to get along at work and everything." She glanced over her shoulder, toward where the professor was bent over a rock ledge, examining something with a jeweler's loupe fitted to his eye. "You're not saying you think he had anything to do with her disappearance?"

He ignored the question. "So Jenny wasn't upset with Eddleston?"

"No!" She stared at him, eyes wide.

"Maybe she was jealous he had gone back to his wife."

"It wasn't like that with them." Another glance at Eddleston. "At least, I don't think so."

"It wasn't like what?"

"Serious. I mean, Jenny was gorgeous, right? And Eddleston, well, no offense, but he sort of reminds me of a plucked chicken."

Ryan bit the inside of his cheek to keep

from smiling at the image, which did, indeed, resemble the professor. "Why did they date, then?" he asked. "Eddleston says she asked him out first."

"I know." Heidi sighed. "It's a mystery to me. I asked her once and she told me she needed someone safe."

Almost the same words Eddleston had used. Words that struck him as odd reasoning from a young woman with a stable life. "What did she mean by that?"

"I don't know. I asked her and she wouldn't explain."

"Do you think she was afraid of something? Or someone?"

"I don't know. Maybe?" She shook her head. "Jenny was always so upbeat, but sometimes—when people are like that all the time—I think maybe it's just a cover-up."

"What do you mean? What are they covering up?"

"They act all cheerful because it keeps people at a distance. Nobody asks too many questions if they think everything is always great. I hope that isn't the case with Jenny, but maybe it was. I mean, I'm her best friend. I should have seen if something was wrong. If I didn't, maybe it was because she was really good at hiding what was really going on."

"Her sister says she didn't pick up on anything, either, and I gather they were close," Ryan said.

"Yeah, they were tight. Jenny really looked up to Jana. But she didn't tell her everything." Her eyes met his, very green and guileless. "You don't, you know, when it's someone you really care about. I mean, I don't tell my parents when there's an accident at work, or a crime in my neighborhood. All it would do is upset them."

"So you think Jenny kept things like that from her sister?"

"Oh, sure."

"What did Jenny keep from me?"

Ryan turned to see Jana striding toward him, her phone in hand. The wind whipped her hair across her face, and she swiped at it with her free hand.

"Hello," Heidi said, the word almost inaudible.

"What was my sister keeping from me?" Jana asked.

"Nothing important, I'm sure," Heidi said. "She didn't want you to worry."

"Worry about what?"

"I don't know. Nothing that I can think of." She looked to Ryan. "Can I go now? I have work I have to finish before we go home for the day."

"Go on," he said. He took Jana's arm and led her a short distance away.

"Did Heidi say Jenny was hiding something from me?" she asked, her expression clouded.

"We were just talking in general, about how people don't tell their loved ones everything because they don't want the people they care about to worry."

"Well, it doesn't work. I'm plenty worried." She thrust the phone at him. "I just found this."

He studied the message on the screen and adrenaline surged through him. "Did you just get this?"

"The date on the message is August tenth— yesterday. The day Jenny disappeared. But I swear, this is the first time I've seen it. It was marked as *read*."

"Did someone else have your phone?"

"No. It must be some glitch. Occasionally I get a message hours after it was sent, or my phone doesn't alert me to a new message. Maybe something like that happened. But look at what it says. She's in trouble. She was trying to tell me she needed help."

Jana was all but vibrating with anxiety, her voice high and strained. He put a hand on her shoulder to steady her. "Even if you had gotten this message when Jenny sent it, you were miles away in Denver," he said.

"Yes, but I could have texted back and asked her what was wrong. I could have called the police."

"Why didn't Jenny call the police?" he asked. "Maybe it wasn't that kind of trouble. Maybe this message doesn't even have anything to do with her disappearance."

She looked at him sharply, irritation replacing some of her agitation. "You don't really believe that, do you?"

"No." He pocketed the phone. "I need to keep this for a while. I'll have our tech guy take a look. Maybe we can determine where it was sent from."

"You can trace Jenny through her phone, can't you?" Her expression brightened. "I think I read something about pings. Have you tried that?"

"We have. But we're not getting anything from her phone."

"Maybe the battery is dead," she said.

"We're still trying everything to locate her." He tapped the phone. "Maybe this will help."

She glanced over her shoulder. "Did Heidi tell you anything useful?"

He hesitated. Discussing a case with a civilian went against all his training.

"I'm her sister!" She squeezed his arm. "I'm going crazy worrying about her. If you know anything that can help me, tell me."

If he knew anything that could take away her pain, he wouldn't hesitate to tell her, but the only thing that would do that was the news that her sister had been found. Still, some information was probably better than the feeling of being kept in the dark. "She confirmed that your sister and Professor Eddleston had a brief affair," he said. "They parted amicably and, according to Heidi, it wasn't a serious relationship."

"Why did she date the man at all?"

"Heidi said Jenny told her the same thing she told Eddleston—that he was safe, or that he made her feel safe."

"I reread all the text messages Jenny sent me since I saw her last," she said. "None of them mentioned Eddleston or Eric Patterson. She didn't talk about dating anyone. And she never mentioned being afraid or unsure, or needing to be 'safe.'"

They reached the cruiser and he held the passenger door open for her. "I'll take a look at the texts, too," he said. "Maybe I'll see something. In the meantime, we'll get you a loaner phone."

She said nothing more until they were well away from the dig site. "I was so upset by the news that Jenny was having an affair with Eddleston that I forgot to tell you something else the women at Daniel Metwater's camp told me," she said.

"What was that?"

"They said they saw Jenny arguing with Eric Patterson. He was calm, but Jenny was apparently really upset."

He tightened his grip on the steering wheel. "When was this?"

"They didn't say. But not the same day one of the women saw Jenny kissing Eddleston." She turned to him. "Do you think it means anything?"

"Hard to say. Couples fight sometimes. I'll question the women again, see if we can put together a timeline. And I'll talk to Eric, too."

She crossed her arms over her chest. "I feel so helpless, sitting in that motel room, not doing anything. What can I do to help?"

His first inclination was to tell her there was nothing she could do—she had to let law enforcement do its job and she couldn't interfere. But he knew how he would react if someone told him that. "Make a list of every one of Jenny's friends that you know of," he said. "Ask them if she talked about going hiking by herself or wanting to explore the area on her own. Find out if she was upset about anything or afraid of anyone."

"I can do that."

"In the meantime, Search and Rescue has a chopper flying the area, looking for any sign of her, and my team is talking to people and looking and putting the word out. If Jenny is out there, we'll find her."

She looked away, silent for a long moment as they left the dirt track and turned onto the paved highway. "Maybe she's not out there," she said softly. "Maybe she's dead."

"I hope that's not the case," he said.

"But when a young woman goes missing— a young woman who wasn't depressed or having money troubles or the type of person to disappear on purpose—when that happens, a lot of them never come back."

He chose his words carefully, not wanting to be dishonest, but also unwilling to upset her unnecessarily. "Cases like that are sometimes victims of violence. I don't know the exact statistics."

"Tell me about the other women you're looking for," she said. "Are they anything like Jenny?"

He didn't see how talking to her about the other women could hurt his case, and she might even have ideas that could help him. "Lucia Raton and Alicia Mendoza," he said. "They are near your sister's age—Lucia is eighteen and Alicia is twenty-five. They were last seen in this area—Lucia in a café a few miles up the road with a man we haven't been able to identify and Alicia with a group of illegal immigrants who were traveling through the wilderness area on foot. But other than that, they don't appear to have anything in common with your sister. Lucia was still in high school and Alicia didn't speak English."

"But three women disappearing within a few weeks in the same area looks like a pattern, doesn't it?" she asked.

"Yes, it does."

"Then it's more important than ever that we figure out what happened to Jenny," she said, her voice taking on a harder edge.

"Why is that?"

"If someone is purposely harming women, we have to stop him," she said. "If I can't save my sister, I have to try to save someone else."

Chapter Six

Jana spent a restless night in the motel, hoping against hope that the phone would ring with news that Jenny had been found alive and safe. The next morning, unable to bear another moment in her room, she retreated to the motel coffee shop. She ordered a cup of coffee, then sat with pen and paper, attempting to make a list of everyone Jenny knew, both here in Montrose and in Denver. After all, it was only a five-hour drive between the two cities, and it was possible someone there knew something that would help the case.

"Mind if I join you?"

A shadow fell across her notebook and she looked up to find Eric Patterson, his hand on the back of the chair across from her.

She opened her mouth to tell him she preferred to be alone, then thought better of it. This man was special to Jenny. She shouldn't miss the opportunity to get to know him better. Maybe one-on-one she would discover what it was her sister saw in him. "Please do," she said.

The chair scraped across the floor as he pulled it out and sat. He wore dark aviator glasses, which he removed and tucked into the neck of his peach-colored polo shirt. Despite not being classically handsome, he did have a kind of boyish appeal, though she found the self-important way he carried himself off-putting. "Any news about Jenny?" he asked.

She shook her head and closed the notebook.

"I haven't discovered anything, either," he said. "The paper asked me to do a story on Lucia Raton and Alicia Mendoza. They wanted me to include Jenny in that group— but I refused."

"Why?"

"Because, although at first glance it might seem that three women who disappear in the same area within a short period of time might be connected, Jenny's circumstances are completely different from the other two."

"I'm not sure I follow," she said.

"Both of the other women were engaged in risky behavior. Lucia was hitchhiking and Alicia was in this country illegally. Whereas,

Jenny was working when she disappeared. She was an educated, smart young woman— not the type to strike up a conversation with a shady stranger or to let herself get into a dangerous situation. She once told me she was a good judge of character and I believe her."

He did seem to know her sister well. "What do you think happened to Jenny?" Jana asked. She leaned toward him, tensed for his answer.

"My first thought was that she wanted a break from work, decided to take a little walk and got lost."

Jana nodded. "That was my first thought, too. But searchers have combed the area around the dig site and they haven't found anything."

"Exactly." He pointed a finger at her, like a lecturer making a point. "That led me to my second theory." He sipped his coffee, his eyes locked to hers, clearly waiting for her to ask about his theory.

If there was less at stake, she would have held her tongue to avoid satisfying his need for attention, but she didn't have time to waste on petty games. "What is your theory?" she asked.

"I think Daniel Metwater or one of his followers abducted her. It's one reason I'm eager to embed myself in the group. I could care less about writing a profile of the man—I want to find Jenny."

"Why do you think Metwater has something to do with her disappearance?" she asked. "You just said Jenny is smart and a good judge of character."

"Yes, but even smart people make mistakes sometimes. And our darling Jenny did have something of a blind spot when it came to the local prophet." He took another long sip of coffee. "You do know she regularly read his blog?"

"I saw it bookmarked on her computer."

"She really fell for all his talk of peace and harmony and living close to nature. I'll admit I teased her about it. It was one of the few things we ever disagreed about. When she found out he and his followers were camping near here, she was determined to see him, so I agreed to go with her."

"You told the Rangers she wouldn't have gone to the camp by herself."

"I didn't think so. But if Metwater or one of his followers came to where she was working and invited her to come with them…" He shrugged. "I'm hoping I can find out more as I research my article."

"I spoke to some women at Metwater's

camp who said they had visited the dig site—more than once," she said.

"See." Eric pointed at her again. "They could have struck up a conversation with Jenny and invited her back to camp, where Metwater got hold of her."

"None of her coworkers mentioned her talking to anyone else that day."

"Maybe they didn't see. The conversation could have happened when Jenny went for a walk out of sight of everyone else."

"The Rangers have already questioned Metwater and his followers," she said.

"Please! One thing anyone who has had much contact at all with Metwater's group knows is that they *hate* the Ranger Brigade. Daniel Metwater has a team of lawyers employed to file formal complaints and request restraining orders against the Rangers for harassing him and his followers. And the boys in brown have made a habit of blaming the Family for anything and everything that goes wrong in the park, though they haven't pinned a single crime on the Prophet."

"If Metwater or one of his people did abduct Jenny, what did they do with her?" Jana asked.

"I don't know." Eric's expression sobered. He pushed aside his coffee cup and grasped Jana's hand. "They may merely be keeping her prisoner, perhaps trying to brainwash her into joining their group. But we have to prepare ourselves for the possibility that she is no longer with us."

Jana wrenched her hand from his grasp. "You mean she might be dead."

He sat back. "It's what the Rangers think, even though they're too politically correct to say so."

Or too kind, Jana thought, remembering Ryan's sympathy. "If you learn something from Metwater that can help the Rangers in their investigation, will you tell them?" she asked.

"That depends on what I find out, and maybe on the timing. I wouldn't wait on the Rangers if I could rescue Jenny myself."

He would like that, wouldn't he, being the big hero? She pushed the uncharitable thought away. "I don't care who saves her, as long as she's safe," she said.

"Of course. That's what I want, too." He reached for her hand once more, but she leaned back, putting herself out of reach. He smiled. "The two of us didn't exactly meet under the best of circumstances, did we?" he said. "I would really like to get to know you better. When Jenny does return to us—and I'm not going to allow myself to think otherwise—I'd like her to know that the two people she loves most in the world are friends."

"Of course." She didn't know if she could ever be close to Eric, but for Jenny's sake, she wanted to be on good terms with him.

"Let me take you to dinner tonight," Eric said. "That will give us a chance to get better acquainted. I can tell you how Jenny and I met."

Yes, that was a story she would like to hear—though she would rather her sister had told her. "Dinner sounds good," she said. "And I am going a little crazy sitting around my motel room, waiting for something to happen."

"Which room is yours? I'll come for you at seven, if that's all right."

"I'll meet you in the lobby at seven."

He grinned. "You remind me so much of Jenny. Our first date she wouldn't let me come to her house, either, but met me at the restaurant."

She could have reminded him this wasn't a date, but why bother?

A movement at the front of the coffee shop caught her attention, and she looked up to see Ryan Spencer silhouetted in the doorway. Her heart sped up as he started toward them. "Looks like that Ranger is here to badger you again," Eric said. "I can get rid of him for you."

He pushed back his chair and started to stand. "Hello, Officer Spencer," Jana said. She made a point of smiling at the Ranger, sending the message that she didn't consider him a nuisance.

Ryan glanced from her to Eric. "Sorry to interrupt," he said.

"You weren't interrupting," she said. "I was just leaving, but you can walk me out." She stood and collected her purse.

"I hope you're not in too much of a hurry," Eric said, rising also and facing Ryan. "I have some questions for you about the missing women—Lucia Raton and Alicia Mendoza."

"I can't discuss details of an ongoing investigation," Ryan said.

"I'm not asking as a civilian. I'm working on a story for the paper."

Ryan looked him up and down. Nothing in his expression betrayed him, but Jana had the sense the reporter didn't impress the lawman. "I thought you were writing a profile of Daniel Metwater," the Ranger said.

"I can work on more than one story at a time. In fact, it's a requirement of the job."

"You're welcome to contact our media liaison," Ryan said. "I don't have anything for you." He stepped aside and motioned to Jana. "I'll walk with you a moment. I just had some news I wanted to share."

"What kind of news?" Eric said.

"The information is for Ms. Lassiter," Ryan said.

"If it's about Jenny, as her fiancé I have a right to know about it," Eric said.

The chill in Ryan's eyes could have frozen water. "The information I have is for Ms. Lassiter." He took Jana's arm. "We won't keep you any longer."

Eric glared at the lawman, hands fisted at his sides. He reminded Jana of a pug faced off against a Doberman. The newspaperman's bluster was no match for Ryan's quiet strength. After a tense moment, Eric turned to Jana. "I'll see you tonight," he said.

Ryan waited until Eric was gone before he spoke. "Do you want to stay and finish your coffee?" he asked.

"I'm done. There's a park on the corner. Could we walk there?"

"Of course."

Sun glared on the sidewalk and sparkled on the fountain in front of the motel. Ryan walked next to the street, matching his strides to Jana's, his quiet presence calming her. When they reached the park, they turned onto a shaded path. "Are you meeting Eric Patterson tonight?" he asked.

"I agreed to have dinner with him," she said. "I didn't really want to, but I felt I should make an effort to be friendly with him, for Jenny's sake."

"He's going to pump you to find out what I had to say to you," he said.

She stopped and faced him. "What *do* you have to say to me?"

"I wanted to return your phone." He took the smartphone from his pocket and handed it to her.

She caressed the sleek silver case. "Did you find anything useful on it?"

"Not really. As far as we can determine, Jenny sent that last text to you from the dig site the morning of the day she disappeared."

"I thought there wasn't any service out there."

"Phone calls don't go through. Most of the time text messages don't, but in a few spots there's enough of a signal to send one. Have you thought any more about what she meant, when she said she had made a mistake?"

Jana shook her head. "I haven't a clue." She opened her purse to drop in the phone and spotted the list she had been making and took it out. "I wrote down the names of people

Jenny knows, both here and in Denver. But I don't know how much help it will be to you." She tore off the page and handed it to him.

He studied the names, then folded the paper and tucked it into his shirt pocket. "I'll have someone check these out. Maybe we'll get lucky and one of these people will know something."

"Do you mind if we walk?" she asked. "I think better when I'm moving."

He fell into step beside her. "The aerial survey of the area didn't turn up anything," he said. "I'm sorry."

"Eric thinks Daniel Metwater or one of his followers abducted Jenny."

"I thought he was a fan of the Prophet. He's writing about Metwater for the paper."

"He told me he's hoping to use his access to Metwater to find Jenny." She glanced at him. In profile he looked less like a carefree surfer and more forbidding, his face all strong planes and sharp angles. "He knew about her following Metwater's blog. He said Jenny was anxious to meet the Prophet, and though they agreed to visit the camp together, if someone from the camp came to the dig and invited her to go back to the camp with them, she would have accepted the invitation. That sounds like Jenny, and we know the women I talked to had visited the dig site at least twice. Maybe they came back the day Jenny disappeared and persuaded her to go with them."

"And what does Eric think happened then?"

"He suggested Metwater was holding her, trying to brainwash her into joining their cult." She pressed her lips together, then forced out the rest of the thought. "Or that she's dead."

"I'll have to review his interview with the sheriff to see if he mentioned any of this to them," Ryan said. "He didn't mention it when we questioned him."

"Maybe he just thought of it," Jana said.

"We're continuing to investigate Metwater, in relation to all the missing women," Ryan said. "We'll certainly question the women you spoke with. I can't say more."

"Eric told me Metwater hates the Rangers—that he thinks they harass him."

"Mr. Patterson knows a lot about the situation."

"He does have a personal interest in the case, and I imagine his job gives him access to a great deal of information."

"Tell him if he finds out anything that could help us, he needs to let us know."

"I already did, though I get the impression he'd like to find Jenny himself and be the hero."

"If she's found safe, I won't complain."

"No ego involved?"

"The day I start thinking an investigation is about me is the day I need to turn in my badge."

She put her hand on his arm, the muscle hard beneath her fingers. "I wasn't questioning your dedication. And I appreciate knowing you're working hard to find Jenny."

He looked down at her hand, then covered it with his own—his touch reassuring but sending a definite heat through her. "How long do you plan on staying in Montrose?" he asked.

"Until I know what happened to my sister."

"We try to solve cases quickly, but, realistically, it could take weeks, or months. Sometimes cases are never solved."

She bowed her head. "I know."

"Don't you have to get back to work?"

"I'm self-employed. I've been able to do some work remotely, but, yes, eventually I'll have to get back to my office or risk losing my clients." She stared out across the park, toward a playground where a trio of children raced about, laughing. "It's hard to concentrate on anything else while I'm so worried about my sister."

"You're entitled to a victim's advocate. I can put you in touch with one."

"What does a victim's advocate do?"

"They're volunteers who liaison with law

enforcement and crime victims or their families. They can also put you in touch with counseling and support groups."

Her shoulders sagged. "So you really think this is a crime?"

"There's still the possibility that your sister wandered off and got lost, but the odds of that seem slim, especially with two other women missing." His grasp on her tightened.

She thought about statistics she had read in the newspaper or heard repeated on television—that the longer a missing person remained unfound, the more likely it was that they were dead. Despair threatened to overwhelm her, but she refused to give in. Instead, she focused on Ryan—on the caring in his eyes and the strength in his grasp. "I want to stay here awhile longer," she said. "And I want to do whatever I can to help."

"Maybe this list will help," he said. "I'll let you know what we find."

His phone rang and he released her. "I need to take this call," he said, and stepped away.

She turned toward the playground again and was reminded of racing Jenny to the top of the slide at the park down the street from the house where they had grown up. Jenny was always the bolder of the two, running faster, climbing higher, teasing Jana with taunts of "slowpoke" and "fraidycat." Jana, though older, had always sought safety, order and control. It was probably why accounting appealed to her. Jenny had always craved adventure, so archaeology was a natural fit.

Had that sense of adventure and daring gotten Jenny into trouble now? Or was she simply the unlucky victim of some nameless evil? She hugged her arms across her middle, trying to ward off the chill that traveled through her despite the warm sun. She had faced some hard things in her life, including the deaths of her parents, but losing Jenny would be the hardest yet.

"Jana?"

She turned at the sound of Ryan's voice, alarm sweeping over her as she registered the distress in his eyes. "What is it?" she demanded. "What's wrong?"

"I'd better go now. I'll talk to you soon."

"I can tell from your expression something bad has happened. Tell me. I promise I won't get hysterical, but I need to know."

He gripped her arms, holding her up. "A road crew found a woman's body near the wilderness area."

Chapter Seven

Ryan led Jana to a bench, afraid she might collapse at any moment. She trembled in his arms, but made it to the bench and sank onto it. "We don't know yet if it's Jenny," he said.

"But it could be," she said, the words coming out in a moan.

"Don't assume anything until we know for sure," he said.

She sucked in a deep breath, fighting for control, and nodded. "What did the caller say?"

"Just that they'd found a body. They're taking it to the coroner's office."

"When will they know who it is?"

"I don't know." He didn't tell her that the body had been found in a shallow grave beside the road, that it had been partially unearthed by animals. The coroner would assess the remains and compare them to the descriptions of the missing women, as well as descriptions of the clothing they had been wearing when last seen.

Jana clutched at his hand. "Don't leave me," she said.

"I won't." He sat beside her. One of the mothers on the playground stared at them. She was probably wondering what he had said to upset Jana so. "Do you want to go back to your room?" he asked.

"Yes. It's too bright out here." She stood.

He didn't ask what she meant by that. Maybe bad news was harder to take on a beautiful, sunny day. He put his arm around her, and together they walked slowly back to the motel and around the side to her room. She fumbled with her key card, so he took it from her and opened the door.

"Can I get you anything?" he asked, as he followed her inside.

"On television, they're always giving people stiff drinks when they've suffered a shock," she said. "But I'm not much of a drinker." She sat on the side of the bed and he took the room's only chair, beside the front window.

He searched for something to distract her and noticed yarn and knitting needles on the nightstand. "What are you working on?" he asked, nodding toward it.

She cradled the ball of soft blue yarn. "I'm knitting a sweater," she said. "I usually find it relaxing, but I don't think I could concentrate on it now." She looked around the room, which was decorated in a country theme, with a floral bedspread and prints of tractors in cornfields on the wall. "What do we do now?" she asked. "Just wait?"

"There's a lot of waiting in my job," he said. "Results rarely happen as quickly in real life as they do on TV."

"I shouldn't keep you," she said. "You have work to do." She smoothed her hands down her thighs. "I'll be fine on my own. And you said you have to go."

He had only said that because he knew if he stayed with her he would tell her the news about the body. Since that cat was already out of the bag, there was no harm in remaining until he was sure she was okay. "I'll stay a little longer." He liked sitting here with her—not the circumstances that had brought them together, but he appreciated the opportunity to be alone with her, to enjoy looking at her. Despite her distress, she was beautiful—not the calendar-girl, cheerleader beauty of her sister, but a more mature, riper attractiveness that drew him.

"Tell me how you became a cop," she said.

He wondered if she was really interested or only searching for distraction. "I did a stint in the army right out of high school, hoping to earn money for college," he said. "After I was discharged, I enrolled in Colorado State University, studying business. At a job fair my senior year I stopped by a booth for Customs and Border Protection. They were looking for officers, and I thought it sounded more interesting than sitting in an office all day."

"And is it? More interesting?"

"Most of the time, yes. I mean, there's a lot of paperwork and waiting for things to happen. It's not all chasing criminals and solving big cases. But I enjoy the variety. And I feel like I'm making a difference."

"What does your girlfriend—or wife—think of the job?"

"I'm not married, or involved."

The corners of her mouth tilted up for the space of a breath. "I wasn't getting a married or involved vibe from you, but you never know."

His gaze met hers and he could almost see the sparks arcing between them. "What kind of vibe are you getting?" he asked.

"One that makes me wonder how often you get involved with women who are part of a case you're working on."

"Never." He continued holding her gaze. "But there's a first time for everything, with the right woman."

She looked away, lamplight playing across the curve of her cheek and the smooth column of her neck. He fought the urge to kiss her there. "This may be the definition of bad timing," she said.

"Probably," he said. "But if everyone waited for life to be perfect no one would ever fall in love or get married or have children or start a new business or take a new job or any of the dozens of big decisions that add up to a full life."

"Yes, but do I feel this attraction to you because there's something between us, or because you're something steady I can hold on to while I'm reeling from my sister's disappearance?"

"I think the only way we're going to learn the answer to that question is to stick around and find out," he said. He stood and came over to sit on the bed beside her. He wasn't going to push her, but he wasn't going to hide his feelings, either. He took her hand. "It depends on what you want."

"I think, right now, I'd like you to kiss me."

"With pleasure." Cradling her cheek in one hand, he covered her lips with his. She tasted faintly of tea and honey, her mouth warm and silken. She slid her hand along his arm and then his shoulder, fingers playing across his skin as if memorizing the shape of him. When he angled his mouth to deepen the kiss, she slid closer, pressing her chest to his, soft curves against hard muscle, quickening his breath and heating his blood.

She opened her mouth beneath his, and he accepted the invitation, the welcome intimacy banishing his last doubts that they might be making a mistake. Her hand slid to the back of his neck and her tongue tangled with his, sending a new wave of pleasure through him. Moments ago, in the park, she had seemed fragile and helpless, but in his arms now she was strong and confident, a woman who knew what she wanted.

The knowledge that she wanted him filled him with desire and more than a little awe.

His ringing phone jarred them apart. Heart pounding, he groped for the cell, fighting to come out of the fog she had put him in. "Spencer."

"We have a positive ID on the body." Commander Graham Ellison's voice was calm and steady.

Ryan turned to Jana, who sat back, fingers pressed to her lips, eyes fixed on him. "Yes?"

"The coroner confirms it's Alicia Mendoza. She was wearing a locket with her name on it, and the clothes fit the description we got from the people she was traveling with."

"Alicia Mendoza," Ryan repeated.

Jana let out a sob and covered her eyes, her shoulders shaking though she made no other sound.

Ryan stood, walked to the window and peered out through a gap in the closed drapes. "Do we know the cause of death yet?"

"She was strangled. Probably at another location, then buried in the shallow grave by the roadside. We'll know more later, but the best estimate right now is that she died within hours of her disappearance."

"I'll be in the office within the hour," Ryan said.

"I want you to meet Simon and Ethan out at Metwater's camp. We've got a warrant to take the place apart."

Ryan felt the familiar jolt of a case gaining momentum. "What are we looking for?" he asked.

"Anything that ties Metwater to Alicia Mendoza or the other missing women. Alicia's hands were bound with white linen fabric, like those shirts and pants Metwater always wears."

RYAN MET ETHAN and Simon at the turnoff for the rough track that led around Mystic Mesa to Metwater's camp. From there they proceeded in two vehicles to the parking area. As soon as they exited their cruisers a beefy young man with a shaved head stepped out to greet them. He hefted a thick wooden walking stick in one hand. "What is your business in our home, officers?" he asked.

"We're here to speak with Daniel Metwater," Simon said.

"The Prophet doesn't allow weapons in the camp," the guard said. "If you'll leave them in your vehicle, I'll be happy to escort you to the Prophet."

"Not happening." Simon shoved past him.

"You don't have to escort us," Ethan said, as he, too, moved past the young man. "We know the way."

Brandishing the walking stick, the young man hurried after them. "The Prophet isn't free to see you right now," he said. "He's in an interview."

Ryan turned to the young man. "You need to put down that stick," he said. "Somebody might get the wrong idea and think you were threatening us with a weapon."

The guard reddened. His gaze flickered to the gun at Ryan's side, then he lowered the walking stick. "The Prophet doesn't like to be interrupted," he said, his tone almost pleading.

"Too bad."

Ryan joined the others at the bottom of the steps leading up to Metwater's motor home. Though the camp seemed deserted, he sensed people watched them from the tents and trailers all around them. Alert to possible danger, he kept one hand near his duty weapon as Simon knocked hard on the aluminum-clad door of the motor home.

He had lifted his hand to knock a second time when the door eased open and Andi Mattheson, aka Asteria, peered out. "The Prophet can't see you right now," she said. "He's in a meeting."

Simon wedged his foot in the narrow opening and pressed his shoulder to the door. "You need to let us in," he said, his voice surprisingly gentle. "Then you should leave. We don't want to see you hurt."

"I don't—" she started to argue.

"Trust me on this." Simon pushed the door open wide enough that he could put both hands on her shoulders. Then he steered her out the door and down the steps. "Wait for us in your tent," he said.

Scowling, she moved past the other two officers and down the steps. "Who knew you had such a way with women?" Ethan said as he and Ryan followed Simon into the motor home.

Metwater sat at the dining table with Eric Patterson across from him. "What are you doing here?" Metwater rose to face them. "Get out of my home."

"Daniel Metwater, we have a warrant to search these premises." Simon laid the warrant on the table in front of Metwater.

"Search for what?" Metwater asked. "By what authority?"

Eric picked up the paper and scanned it. "By the authority of the Seventh Judicial District Court," he said. "It looks official."

"Mr. Patterson, what are you doing here?" Ryan asked.

"I'm interviewing the Prophet for the profile of him I'm writing," he said.

"You'll have to finish the interview some other time," Simon said. "You need to leave now."

"Oh no," Eric said. "I need to stay. Things are just about to get interesting."

"Leave, or I'll detain you for interfering with an investigation," Simon said.

"Mr. Metwater is entitled to have someone

with him as a witness," Eric said. He turned to Metwater. "You want me to stay, don't you?"

"You're making that up," Simon said. "There's no requirement for a witness."

"I'm sure I read it somewhere," Eric said. "What if you're wrong and I'm right? The Rangers don't need any more bad publicity, do they?" He sat back and folded his arms. "Besides, if you end up charging Mr. Metwater with something and the case goes to trial, I'm an outside witness who can testify to what you find. That would look good to a jury, don't you think?"

The tips of Simon's ears were bright red, and Ryan could practically see the irritation radiating from him. Ethan put a hand on Simon's shoulder. "Quit wasting time with him," he said. "Let's get on with the search."

Simon shrugged off Ethan's hand and turned back to Metwater. "Do you know Alicia Mendoza?" he asked.

"I've never heard of her," Metwater said.

"Alicia is the Mexican woman who went missing near here," Eric said. "You remember I was telling you about her."

Metwater glared at him.

"She was from Guatemala, not Mexico,"

Ryan said. He took Eric's arm. "You and Mr. Metwater need to wait outside."

"I want to talk to my lawyer," Metwater said.

"Go right ahead." Simon took his arm. "You can call him from Ms. Mattheson's tent, provided you can get a cell signal out here. I don't think you can, but you're welcome to try."

Metwater shook him off, but stood and started toward the door.

"You have to leave, too," Ethan told Eric.

"I could stay and help you," Eric said. "If you tell me what you're looking for."

"Out," Simon said. He waited for the reporter to move past him, then fell into step behind him. "I'll keep an eye on these two and Ms. Mattheson," he said. "Let me know if you find anything interesting."

When they were alone, Ethan turned to Ryan. "You want to take Metwater's bedroom? I'll look in here, then we'll hit the other rooms."

Ryan pulled on a pair of latex gloves and went to work. Starting to the left of the bedroom door, he circled the room clockwise, opening every drawer, feeling along every surface, riffling through books and looking behind pictures. He stripped the bed and searched between the mattress and box spring, then emptied the drawer of the bedside table. Metwater had a good supply of condoms and an assortment of sex toys in these drawers. His reading material was a mix of investment advice and the writings of eastern mystics. Maybe he was copying ideas for his blog posts from them. A notebook was filled with notes made in an almost indecipherable handwriting. Ryan bagged and tagged this to be reviewed at Ranger headquarters.

The dresser held a collection of white cotton or linen trousers and shirts, some silk pajama pants, underwear and socks. The closet held half-a-dozen expensive-looking suits and as many pairs of shoes. Ryan was about to shut the door and move on to another room when something white at the very back of the space caught his eye. He squatted and played his flashlight across the floor of the closet. A heap of white fabric, like a shirt that had slipped from a hanger, lay wadded in the very back corner of the space. Ryan pulled it out and stared at what once had been a shirt, but was now little more than a rag. The fabric had been cut and torn, so that long strips hung from the shoulders, and about half of it looked to be missing.

"Ethan!" he called. "Come take a look at this."

His fellow Ranger appeared in the doorway. "What have you got?" he asked.

Ryan held up the torn shirt. "I think we've found what we were looking for."

Chapter Eight

Jana couldn't believe Eric Patterson had stood her up. She had waited in the lobby of her motel from five minutes before seven until seven thirty and the reporter never showed. By that time she had read every brochure in the tourist-information rack by the door and played fourteen games of solitaire on her phone. He hadn't even had the decency to call and cancel. What had Jenny seen in the guy?

Starving and furious, she drove to a sandwich shop and placed an order to go, then took it to Jenny's apartment. If Eric did decide to finally show up at the motel, she was in no mood to talk to him. She called Jenny's roommate, April, from the parking lot. "I'm sorry to bother you," Jana said. "But would it be okay if I came up for a while?"

"Uh, sure," April said, sounding very unsure.

"I have to leave in a little bit to meet a friend for drinks, but you still have a key, right?"

"I do. And thanks. I promise I'll be gone by the time you get home."

She followed April into the apartment and sat in a chair while April settled on the couch. She was a petite Asian American with short black hair streaked with purple. "Any word on how the search is going?" April asked.

"Nothing yet." She started to tell April about Alicia Mendoza's body being found, but why put worry about a connection between the missing Guatemalan woman and Jenny in April's head if it wasn't already there? "I know the Rangers are working hard to find her," she said, instead.

"They're bound to turn up something soon, right?" April said.

"April, did Jenny seem upset about anything in the days before she disappeared?" Jana asked.

"The cops asked me the same thing. But, no, Jenny wasn't upset." She smoothed her hands down her thighs. "We didn't really see each other that much, you know. We were both really busy with work and studies and stuff."

"Did you know Jenny was dating two different guys?" Jana asked.

"I knew she had a pretty active social life,

but she didn't talk about her dates, much. Well, except I knew Eric. He was over here pretty often."

"Did you know he and Jenny were engaged?"

"He told me one day when he came to pick up Jenny, while she was in the bathroom getting ready. But he said it had to be a secret until they had a chance to tell you."

"Were you surprised?" Jana asked.

April wrinkled her nose. "A little. I mean, I didn't really think Jenny was that into him. I was going to ask her about it the next time we were alone, but I never got the chance."

There were so many things Jana wanted to ask her sister, too. The thought of never having that opportunity was a constant dull ache in the pit of her stomach.

April stood. "I have to go now. But you can hang out as long as you like."

"Thanks," Jana said. "Sometimes it helps being here, where I feel a little closer to her."

After April had left, Jana retrieved her supper from the car and carried it up to the apartment. Bypassing the living room and kitchen, she went to Jenny's room. At the desk, she switched on Jenny's laptop, and arranged her food beside it. The screen saver popped up—a picture of a smiling Jenny, Eric standing next to and slightly behind her. Jana stared at the image. She would have sworn it hadn't been there two days ago when she was here. She and Ryan had both commented on the lack of photos of Jenny and Eric on the computer.

She clicked on the icon for Jenny's photo album. The page filled with thumbnails of her sister—alone, with friends—and with Eric. Enlarging one image, Jana studied a picture of Eric with his arm around a solemn-faced Jenny. The shot had been taken out of doors, possibly at the dig site. Though Eric was grinning broadly, Jenny looked unhappy about something.

Other images in the file were of Eric by himself. One looked like the kind of head-shot that might run with a newspaper column while others resembled selfies taken in front of local landmarks, such as the painted canyon walls in Black Canyon of the Gunnison National Park. But none of these images had been on Jenny's laptop when Jana had looked two days before.

She was trying to puzzle this out when her cell phone rang. The number was local, but not one she knew. "Hello?" she answered, cautious.

"Jana, it's Eric. I'm sorry I couldn't make dinner tonight. I would have called earlier, but

I was out at Daniel Metwater's camp, with no cell service. I swung by the motel to apologize in person, but you weren't there."

"I'm sure your story on him was more important than dinner with me," she said, hoping he noted the sarcasm in her voice.

"It wasn't that. I planned to finish up in plenty of time to meet you, but the Rangers showed up and I didn't dare leave."

"The Rangers? Which Rangers?"

"Ryan Spencer and a couple of others. They had a warrant to search Daniel Metwater's motor home. I was in the motor home with Metwater when they arrived."

"And they asked you to stay?"

"No, but I would have been crazy to leave. Good thing I didn't, or I would have missed out on the biggest story of my career."

He sounded so excited—gleeful, even. "What happened?" she asked.

"The Rangers have arrested Daniel Metwater—for murder."

"Whose murder?" She had to force out the words, her tongue frozen along with the rest of her.

"For the murder of the woman whose body they found this afternoon—the one from Mexico or Guatemala or wherever it was. Apparently, Metwater killed her."

"The Rangers *think* he killed her," Jana clarified.

"Right. But they wouldn't have arrested him if they didn't think they had pretty solid proof. I hope this isn't too upsetting for you. Where are you?"

"I stopped by Jenny's apartment."

"Are you there by yourself? You probably shouldn't be alone at a time like this."

A time like what? "I'm fine," she said.

"That's good to know. I have to go now. I have to write up this story and get it in tomorrow's edition. I'm thinking front page. This is big!"

The call ended before she could say another word. Jana stared at her phone, trying to absorb this news.

With shaking fingers, she punched in Ryan's number. He answered on the fourth ring. "Hello, Jana," he said, his voice warm and friendly, as if he was pleased to hear from her.

"Did you really arrest Daniel Metwater for Alicia Mendoza's murder?" she asked.

"Who told you that?" he asked, all the warmth vanishing from his voice.

"Eric Patterson called me."

He muttered what might have been a curse. "Yes, it's true," he said.

"Have they found anything to link Metwater to Jenny?"

"Nothing so far. I'm sorry, I have to go. I'll talk to you later."

The contrast between the two men struck her—Eric so energized and gleeful at the news of Metwater's arrest, Ryan weary and maybe a little sad. "Try to get some rest sometime," she said.

"You, too."

The call ended, and Jana sat, the silence of the empty apartment closing in around her. She thought of so many questions she should have asked Ryan. The Rangers thought Daniel Metwater had murdered Alicia Mendoza. Did they believe he had something to do with Jenny's disappearance, as well? Could they force him to tell them what had happened to Jenny? Was this the break they needed to find her sister?

If they found Jenny, would she still be alive? Every hour that passed without hearing from her seemed to increase the probability that Jana would never see her sister alive again.

She pushed the thought away and shut down Jenny's computer. Time to get out of here. At the motel she would take a long hot shower, then find a movie to stream—something cheerful and unchallenging, to take her mind off all the things around her over which she had no control.

She cleaned up the remains of her supper, wrote a note for April thanking her for letting her hang out in Jenny's room for a while, then left, making sure to lock up behind her.

It was almost ten o'clock, and clouds had moved in to obscure the moon. The parking lot was so dark that Jana thought about pulling out her phone and turning on the flashlight app. But she only had to walk a few yards to her car and didn't want to take the time to fumble with her phone. Instead, she took out her keys and clicked the button to unlock her car.

The headlights winked at her and she relaxed a little. She'd have no trouble making her way safely to the car now. Walking quickly, she moved toward the driver's-side door. What movie should she watch tonight? Was she in the mood for a comedy, or was a good love story the best thing to distract her?

She was reaching for the door handle when a pair of strong arms encircled her, crushing her ribs and lifting her off the ground. Then pain exploded at the back of her head and the world went black.

Ryan studied the man who sat across from him in the interview room at the Montrose police station. Ranger headquarters had no facility for holding prisoners, so they had brought Metwater here for questioning and detainment until he was either bailed out or held over for trial. Metwater didn't so much sit in the chair as balance there, like a panther readying himself to pounce. A pulse throbbed at his temple, and the muscles along his jaw knotted. His long, elegant fingers curled and uncurled into fists.

Ethan tossed the torn shirt onto the table in front of Metwater. "Does this belong to you?" he asked.

Metwater scarcely glanced at the garment. "It's a rag. It could belong to anybody."

"We found it in your closet. Check the label."

"I want my lawyer. I refuse to do anything without counsel present."

"Suit yourself," Ethan said. "I'll read the label to you." He lifted the collar of the shirt and squinted at the label. "Balenciaga. The same label as six other shirts like this that we found in your motor home."

Metwater stared at them, silent.

"You're living pretty large for a humble prophet," Ethan said. "I did a little research and these shirts retail for over two hundred dollars each. Not the kind of thing most guys have in their closets."

Metwater remained stone-faced.

Ethan glanced at Ryan, who had been leaning against the doorjamb. Ryan straightened and joined his partner at the table. "Highway workers found Alicia Mendoza's body this afternoon," he said. "She was strangled with strips of fabric cut from a shirt like this. We're pretty confident tests are going to show the fabric was cut from this shirt. They'll probably have your DNA in them. Why don't you make it easier on yourself and tell us now what happened."

Metwater continued to glare at them. If it were possible for a gaze to burn through someone, Ryan would be full of smoldering holes from Metwater's laser stare.

"Maybe Alicia came to your camp because she was curious, or because she needed help," Ethan said. "You invited her in. You wanted to get to know her better. One thing led to another and maybe she refused your advances, or maybe things got a little rougher than you intended. Maybe it was an accident. Whatever, she ended up dead, and you did the only thing you could do—you got rid of the body."

"If I killed her, why would I be stupid

enough to leave evidence like this shirt lying around?" Metwater asked.

"You were probably pretty upset and stressed-out," Ryan said. "You forgot. It could happen to anyone."

"It didn't happen," Metwater said.

Ryan leaned over Metwater. He could smell the sweat beneath the expensive cologne. "Alicia is dead," he said. "Someone killed her. Who would do that—with your shirt?"

Metwater looked away, shutting them out.

Ryan straightened. "Put him in the cell until his lawyer gets here," he said.

An officer cuffed Metwater and led him away. As he was leaving, Ranger commander Graham Ellison slipped into the interview room. "His lawyer is going to fight us hard on this one," he said.

"Even the best lawyer can't explain away that shirt," Ryan said. "The fabric used to strangle Alicia Mendoza is going to match, I'm sure of it."

"The shirt looks significant, but it may not be enough to hold him," Graham said. "We haven't been able to get anyone to admit to seeing Alicia in Metwater's camp, and half a dozen of his followers swear he never left the camp the day she disappeared and was supposedly killed."

"What about his car?" Ethan asked. "Alicia's body got to that ditch in a vehicle. Maybe we could find DNA evidence in Metwater's car."

"He doesn't have a car," Graham said. "When he needs to go somewhere, someone else drives him. And, again, everyone swears he never left the camp."

"Have we found anything to link him to Lucia Raton or Jennifer Lassiter?" Ryan asked.

"We know Lucia was in his camp at one point, and Jennifer followed his blog," Ethan said. "A jury might see that as significant."

"I can guarantee a defense lawyer would argue it isn't," Graham said.

"What about the three women themselves?" Ethan asked. "Any connections between them?"

"None," Graham said. "Though it seems as if three women who go missing from the same area in the same brief period of time would be connected, we don't have anything concrete to tie them together."

Ryan's phone buzzed. He checked the screen, but the number didn't look familiar, so he silenced it. "We should put some pressure on Andi Mattheson," he said. "She's closest to Metwater. If he's involved in these missing women, she'll know."

"She's completely loyal to him," Ethan said. "I don't think she's likely to betray him."

"We could play up the jealousy angle," Ryan said. "No matter how loyal she is, she won't like it if he's hitting on other women." His phone buzzed again.

"Maybe you'd better take that call," Ethan said.

"Go ahead," Graham said. "Then go home. I don't think there's anything more we can do here tonight."

"Maybe we'll catch a break tomorrow," Ethan said.

Ryan moved into the hallway and pulled out his phone. The screen showed the same unfamiliar number. "Hello?"

"Officer Spencer?" The female voice sounded young and nervous.

Ryan tensed. "Yes."

"This is April Pham. Jenny Lassiter's roommate. Jana Lassiter asked me to call you."

Ryan gripped the phone so hard his fingers ached. "Is something wrong?"

"Someone attacked Jana outside my apartment tonight," April said, her voice wavering. "I came home in time to scare them away. She's here at the hospital."

Ryan didn't need to hear more. He pulled out his keys and ran toward the door. "I'm on my way."

Chapter Nine

Jana squinted in the glare of the bright light overhead and tried not to think about how much her head ached. The sharp odor of antiseptic stung her nose and she shivered in the blast from the air-conditioning, despite the blanket a nurse had spread over the gurney. "Paging Dr. Kitten. Paging Dr. Kitten." The announcement cut through the low-level emergency-room chatter, and Jana fought back an unexpected giggle. Was it tough to gain respect from your patients and colleagues when your name was Dr. Kitten? Or maybe Dr. Kitten was warm and approachable, in keeping with the name.

The doctor who had examined Jana was brisk and businesslike. Jana had a concussion and some bruising. "You should be fine in a few days, maybe a few weeks. Follow up with your primary-care doctor as soon as possible," he said, before hurrying away to his next patient.

The curtain around Jana's cubicle rattled as it slid back, and she turned toward the sound, regretting the movement as soon as she made it. She winced at the fresh stab of pain and Ryan hurried to her side. "Is something wrong?" he asked. "Should I call someone?"

"I'm fine." She managed a weak smile—it really didn't do justice to how glad she was to see him. "What are you doing here?"

"April Pham called me."

"I didn't mean for her to get you out so late. What time is it?"

"Almost one. How are you doing?" He gripped the edge of the gurney.

"I'm okay. Well, except for a headache." She reached out her free hand—the one without the IV—and grasped his fingers.

His grip was strong and somehow managed to convey both his concern and his relief. "Do you remember anything about what happened?" he asked.

"Not much. I was leaving Jenny's apartment, walking to my car, and I guess someone hit me on the head. I blacked out. The next thing I knew, I woke up in the ambulance. I still don't know how I ended up here."

"April told the officers on the scene that

when she arrived home, she heard a woman cry out, then saw a man and woman struggling. She shouted at them and pulled out her phone, and the man fled. She ran over and was surprised to find it was you."

"Thank God she showed up when she did. I don't even want to think about what might have happened if she hadn't."

He squeezed her hand more tightly. "Did you get a look at the guy at all?" he asked.

"No. He came up from behind me. I never saw him at all. Did April see anything?"

"No. It was too dark. What were you doing at Jenny's apartment?"

She grimaced, even though the movement intensified the throbbing in her head. "Eric Patterson and I were supposed to have dinner," she said. "He stood me up and I was annoyed. So I went to Jenny's place. If she had been there, we would have laughed about the whole thing. Instead, I had to settle for being in the place where I feel closest to her." She tried to blink back the tears that filled her eyes, but one slipped down her cheek.

Ryan wiped the tear away gently. He didn't say anything, but the gesture spoke volumes and brought forth a fresh flow of tears.

She was doubly grateful when he pretended

not to notice. "Eric was at Daniel Metwater's camp this afternoon," he said.

"He told me later when he called. That's the excuse he gave for missing dinner with me— that he had to wait to see what the Rangers found when they searched Metwater's motor home." She sniffed and wiped at her eyes with her fingers. He handed her a tissue and she smiled her thanks. "I still can't believe you arrested Metwater," she said. "Do you really think he killed Alicia?"

"We have evidence that suggests that, but nothing that links him to Jenny."

The fact that he even mentioned her sister told Jana he had been thinking along those lines. "I found something a little odd on Jenny's laptop when I was there this evening," she said. "Nothing that relates to her disappearance, I don't think, just something that struck me as strange."

"What was that?"

"Do you remember we talked about how it was weird that she didn't have any pictures of Eric on her computer or her social-media pages, even though they were engaged?"

"Yes."

"I didn't check her social media, but now her computer has all kinds of pictures of

Eric—with her and by himself. I'm sure they weren't there the other night."

"I didn't see any pictures of him when I examined the computer."

"Do you think April could have put them there?" she asked. "But why would she do that?"

He pulled out his phone. "Why don't we ask her?"

Ryan put the phone on speaker so Jana could hear the conversation. After answering April's questions about Jana, Ryan told her the reason for his call. "Did you put any pictures onto Jenny's laptop in the last couple of days?" he asked.

"I haven't touched her laptop," April said, clearly shocked by the idea. "I mean, I would never mess with a roommate's belongings. Why are you asking?"

"Jana was looking at the laptop tonight and found some pictures that she hadn't seen on there before—pictures of Jenny and Eric, and some of Eric by himself."

"I didn't put them there," April said.

"Do you have any idea how they might have got there?" Ryan asked.

"I don't know," she said. "I mean—he was her fiancé. Maybe they were there all along and Jana just didn't see them before. Maybe she didn't open that file or something."

"The police didn't find any of these pictures when we went over the unit, either," Ryan said.

"Weird," April said. "I'm sorry I can't help you."

"Has anyone else—besides you and Jana—been in Jenny's room in the last couple of days?" Ryan asked.

She hesitated. "Well, Eric stopped by here yesterday morning. He said he needed to get a jacket he had left in Jenny's closet. The police told me they were through with the room, so I thought it would be all right to let him go in there."

"You didn't do anything wrong," Ryan reassured her. "Did he get the jacket?"

"He said he couldn't find it."

"How long was he in the room?" Ryan asked.

"Not long. A few minutes, maybe. I was watching TV and I didn't time him or anything."

"Thanks, April," Ryan said. "I appreciate your help." He ended the call and pocketed the phone.

"Why would Eric bother to add pictures to Jenny's computer?" Jana asked.

"I'm going to ask him," Ryan said. "And I'm going to find out where he was this evening after he left Metwater's camp."

"When he called me, he said he was working on his story about Metwater's arrest," she said. "He said he had a deadline to meet to get the story in tomorrow's—well, I guess now it's today's—paper. He sounded really excited about it."

"I still want to know where he was." His grim expression made her glad she wasn't Eric Patterson. Then a chill ran through her. "Ryan, you don't think Eric Patterson attacked me, do you? Why would he?"

"I don't know. But someone attacked you and I want to find out who. Patterson seems a logical place to start."

Nothing about this whole situation seemed logical to Jana, but knowing Ryan was looking out for her made her emotional all over again. She was grateful when a nurse bustled into the room. "Now that your ride is here we can see about discharging you," she said. "I have some instructions for you." She turned to Ryan. "She's not to be left alone tonight. And call and report if you see anything unusual— slurred words, blurred vision, unsteady gait, things like that."

"I'll stay with her," he said. "And I'll call if there are any problems."

"Ryan, I can't ask you to do that," Jana protested.

"I'm staying." His tone told her there was no use arguing.

"Thank you," she said, as he helped her sit up.

She listened to the nurse's instructions, signed the papers she was handed, then was left alone long enough to change back into her clothes. A few minutes later, Ryan wheeled her out of the emergency department to his cruiser. "I could have walked," she said as he helped her stand.

"But you didn't have to." He saw her into the passenger seat and handed her her purse. She stared at the bag in her lap. "Do you think it's strange the guy who hit me didn't take my purse?" she asked.

"Maybe April scared him off before he could grab it." He walked around the vehicle and slid into the driver's seat. "Or maybe he wasn't interested in the purse."

"Which means what? He was interested in me?"

"Three women have mysteriously disappeared in this area in the past three weeks."

Ryan started the cruiser. "And we know one of them is dead."

Her stomach lurched and she bit the inside of her cheek, trying to regain her composure. "I don't think this is related," she said. "How could it be?"

"It may not be, but part of my job is looking at a case from every angle."

"Right." She folded her hands in her lap and stared straight ahead. Her head still throbbed, but less than it had earlier. Mainly, she felt exhausted. She wanted to crawl into bed and forget about all of this for the next ten hours or so.

Sleep. Where was Ryan going to sleep? Her motel room didn't have a sofa. It wasn't even a very large room. "Maybe you should take me to Jenny and April's apartment," she said. "I could stay there tonight. I'm sure April wouldn't mind."

"I'm taking you to my place," he said. "I want you where I can keep an eye on you."

"Oh." She wanted to object that he didn't need to go to so much trouble, but the thought of spending the night alone held no appeal. "Thank you," she said, instead.

"I'll swing by the motel so you can get your things," he said.

Right. She would need "things"—toiletries,

her night gown and a change of clothes. Trying to think of everything made her head hurt.

She closed her eyes and surrendered to the soothing hum of tires on pavement, until the cruiser slowed for the turn into the motel parking lot. "My room's around back," she said. "Number 118."

"I remember."

Right. How could she have forgotten he had been in her room? Though the kiss they had shared now seemed so long ago.

He pulled into a vacant space across from her room and they climbed out of the car. She made no objection when he took her arm. Whether from shock and pain or the late hour, weariness dragged at her. She fumbled in her purse and found her key card. Her fingers brushed against her car keys. "My car—"

"We'll see to it in the morning," he said. "Don't worry about it now. Let me see your room key."

She handed him the card and he started to insert it in the slot, then stopped.

"What is it?" she asked. "What's wrong?"

"This lock has been tampered with." He shifted so that more light fell on the door, and pointed to gouges around the key slot and the knob. He took a handkerchief from his pocket and tried the knob. It turned easily and the door swung open. "Let me go in first," he said.

She nodded, too stunned to speak. He drew his weapon and eased around the door while Jana held her breath. A few moments later he emerged. "It's all right," he said. "It doesn't look as if anyone has been in here."

She moved past him into the room, which looked the same as when she had left it. Ryan took her suitcase from the closet and opened it on the bed. "Pack everything," he said. "You're not coming back here."

She didn't have the strength to argue, and she moved to the dresser and began emptying everything into the suitcase. Ryan disappeared into the bathroom and emerged with her makeup case and hairbrush. "I'll call in a report once I have you settled," he said. "And I'll notify the motel management and get someone out to question staff and guests, in case anyone saw anything."

When she had packed everything, he stashed her suitcase in the back of the cruiser, then helped her into the passenger seat. She willed herself not to think about what had happened, though the image of the violated door played in a loop in her head.

Ryan lived in one of a row of duplexes on the north side of Montrose. The house was plain but clean and comfortable. He led her to a bedroom at the back and set her suitcase on the floor. "The bathroom is across the hall. I'll get some sheets for the bed." He turned to go, but she put out a hand to stop him.

"Don't leave me just yet," she said.

"Of course."

She hesitated, then moved into his arms. "Just hold me," she said. "I don't feel as frightened when you hold me."

His arms encircled her, warm and strong. No one could get to her here—not the man who had attacked her in the parking lot or whoever had vandalized her motel room door. She closed her eyes and rested her head on Ryan's shoulder, and she was too tired and weak to hold back the sob that rose in her throat.

"It's okay," he murmured, and smoothed his hand over the back of her head. "You're safe now."

"I'm so scared," she said. "I could have died tonight."

His arm tightened around her. "You didn't die. I'll find whoever did this. I won't let him hurt you."

She raised her head to look at him, the compassion in his eyes bringing on a fresh flood. "I'm not only scared for myself," she said between sobs. "I'm beginning to think I'm never going to see Jenny again. What if she's dead?"

He cradled her head in his hand. "You'll get through it," he said. "It will be awful, but you'll get through it. I'll help you."

She nodded. He couldn't bring back her sister or lessen the pain news of her death would bring, but she believed he would stay with her, and, for now, knowing that was enough.

"Do you want to come with me to get the sheets for your bed?" he asked.

"I don't want sheets for my bed," she said. "I want to stay with you tonight. I just… I don't want to be alone."

"All right." He picked up her suitcase. "I won't leave you."

He led the way to his bedroom, a larger room furnished with a king-size bed. "You can change in there," he said, indicating a door that led to a large master bath.

She found her nightgown in the suitcase and changed out of her clothes in the bathroom. The sight of a brown stain on her blouse made her stomach heave when she realized it was her own blood. She balled up the blouse so the stain didn't show and focused on washing her face and brushing her teeth, without looking too long at herself in the mirror. The glimpses she allowed showed a pale woman who hardly looked like herself.

She returned to the bedroom to find Ryan already in bed. Weariness overcoming awkwardness, she crawled under the covers. He switched off the light and she lay still, her back to him. Then he moved toward her and his arm came around her. "Is this all right?" he asked.

"Yes." She settled against him, her head cradled in the hollow of his shoulder. "It's more than all right." For tonight, at least, being with him was going to hold back the fear and pain that threatened to overtake her.

Chapter Ten

Ryan lay awake for a long time, too aware of
the feel of Jana against him, the softness of
her body and the scent of her hair to sleep. He
wanted her, but her very vulnerability held
him in check. She needed his protection now
more than she needed his passion.

He rose early and left her sleeping. Staying
with her until she woke would be too much
of a temptation. He was in the kitchen drinking his first cup of coffee when she came in,
dressed but pale, anxiety haunting her eyes.
"How are you feeling this morning?" he
asked, as he took another cup from the cabinet by the stove.

"A little steadier." She accepted the cup, but
avoided looking directly at him. "I'm sorry I
was so clingy last night," she said.

"I have no complaints."

Her cheeks flushed pink, and he wanted to

gather her into his arms and kiss away her embarrassment. But now wasn't the time. "While you were changing last night I called in a report on the forced lock on your motel room," he said. "We'll check it for fingerprints, but I'm not expecting we'll find much."

"This morning, I just want to get my car back," she said. "Can you take me by Jenny's apartment before you go in to work?"

"I'll do that. But for now, I don't want you driving anywhere by yourself," Ryan said.

She opened her eyes and looked him in the eye for the first time that morning. "The doctor didn't say anything about not driving."

"No. But the vandalism of your room makes me think the attack on you last night wasn't random. Someone is targeting you. I'm not going to give them a chance to get to you."

"Who would want to hurt me?" she asked.

"I don't know. But until we find out, I don't want you going anywhere alone." He dumped the dregs of his cup in the sink and set the cup on the drain board. "I'll take you by to get your car, then I have to go in to work, but I've called a friend to come and stay with you this morning."

She frowned. "Another cop?"

"No. But she's married to a cop." He turned his back to her and opened a cabinet. "Do you

want some breakfast? I've got cereal or frozen waffles."

"I don't really feel like eating," she said. "I
just want to get my car."

He turned back to her and pulled her close.
"I know it's a lot to take in," he said. "I wish
I could make it easier for you."

"You make it easier just by being here."

They stood that way for a long moment,
arms wrapped around each other. He breathed
in the floral scent of her hair and savored
the feel of her against him. He wished he
could prolong this interlude, but every minute counted in the hunt for a killer, so after
a while, he reluctantly pulled away. "Let's
get your car," he said. "Then you can meet
Emma."

"Emma?"

"Emma Ellison. You two can hang out
today. You'll like her, I think."

Jana was grateful Ryan didn't press her
to make conversation on the drive from his
place to Jennifer's apartment. Her head ached
and her stomach churned as she tried to process everything that had happened in the
last twelve hours. The attack had been awful
enough when it had seemed like a random
mugging, but seeing the damage to the lock
on her hotel room had shaken something at

her core. She had never in her life not felt safe. Now, nothing about her life felt dependable.

She glanced over at the man in the driver's seat of the cruiser. Except Ryan. She could depend on him, she was sure of it. She wasn't sure she liked relying so heavily on someone else, but she was more than grateful that he was with her now. Last night, lying in his arms, she had felt so protected and safe. So... cherished.

Sleeping together might have led to more, but the timing had been all wrong. Too many bad things were happening—how could they help but color anything good that might happen between her and Ryan?

After today, she would be better, she told herself. She would spend the day with this Emma person and regain her equilibrium. Maybe Ryan would find out what happened to Jenny. Even if it was bad news—terrible news—at least she would know. That would be better, right?

She blinked back tears. Who was she kidding? How could anything but finding Jenny safe and alive be better?

Ryan pulled into the parking lot of the apartment building. "I'm parked over there," she said, indicating a group of visitor's spaces on the far side of the lot.

He parked in an empty space and they got out of the cruiser. "Which car is yours?" Ryan asked, taking her arm.

Something in his voice made her tense and look around. She gasped as her gaze fell on her Jeep, parked a few spaces over and behind them. The front windshield was shattered. "Oh no," she moaned.

Ryan released his hold on her and strode toward the vehicle. She followed, a fresh wave of shock rocking her as she saw that the driver's-side window was broken, as well, and someone had slashed the upholstery, stuffing spilling from the deep cuts. She steadied herself with one hand on the hood. "Who would do this?" she whispered.

Ryan scanned the lot. "I don't see any other cars damaged," he said.

She swallowed hard, a sour taste in her mouth. "You mean someone targeted *my* car," she said.

He took her arm again, and at the same time pulled out his phone. "I'll get a team over here right away to go over the car," he said. "Maybe we'll get lucky and find something."

"He must have come back, after the ambulance took me away, and done this," Jana said. She stared at the damaged car, icy fear spreading through her. The broken windshield was traumatic enough, but the slashed seats felt much more personal. There was anger behind those cuts—hatred.

Ryan ended one call and made another, then turned back to her. "We'll canvass the people in the apartments," he said. "Maybe someone saw or heard something. In the meantime, Emma is on her way over to pick you up."

Jana nodded, numb. Ryan put his hand on her shoulder and looked her in the eye. "I know this is rough," he said. "But you have to pull yourself together. Don't let this guy defeat you. Stay strong—for Jenny."

She nodded and took a deep breath. "Right." She couldn't afford to fall apart now. "Whoever did this hurt my car, but they didn't get me," she said. "I won't let them beat me." Instead of sitting around feeling sorry for herself, she would do whatever she could to try to find the man responsible for this—who maybe was linked to Jenny's disappearance. She wouldn't let him get away without being punished.

EMMA ELLISON WAS the kind of woman who couldn't help but make an entrance. Over six feet tall in heels, her formfitting jeans and sweater accentuated her generous curves. Add in a mane of white-blond curls and rhinestone-trimmed sunglasses and she looked more like an A-list star than a cop's wife. When Ryan had called Commander Ellison last night to report the attack on Jana and her car, Emma had insisted on staying with Jana while Ryan was at work, and her husband had seconded the suggestion, making it all but an order—an order Ryan was happy to follow.

She sped into the apartment parking lot in a bright red sports car and everyone in the area stopped what they were doing and watched her step out of the car. "Hello, Ryan," she said, sweeping past him on a wave of floral perfume. "And you must be Jana. I'm Emma." She thrust a tall paper cup into Jana's hand. "I hope you like caramel lattes. It's my personal favorite. Oh, and I brought muffins." She waggled a white paper bag. "None of these bachelors ever have anything very appetizing for breakfast."

"Thanks." Jana's smile almost reached her eyes.

"Emma is married to my commander, Graham Ellison," Ryan said. "She's a reporter."

"I cover the Western Slope for the *Denver Post*," Emma said. She waved at Ryan in a dismissive gesture. "You can go to work now, Officer. Jana and I have things to discuss."

"What things?" he asked.

Emma widened her eyes. "We're going to talk about you, of course."

RYAN'S GOODBYE WAS BRIEF, perhaps because Emma had her gaze fixed on him. Jana wanted to throw her arms around his neck and kiss him, and maybe thank him again for all he had done for her, but she had to settle for a brief squeeze of his hand as he murmured, "See you later."

When he was gone, she let Emma lead her to the car. Emma settled her drink in the cup holder, fastened her seat belt, and regarded Jana thoughtfully. "Let's take a drive out toward the lake first, enjoy our breakfast and get to know each other better, then we'll come up with a plan for the day."

"I appreciate your taking the time to come get me," Jana said. "But really, I'll be fine on my own. If you could just take me by Ryan's to get my things, then maybe some place to rent a car?" She couldn't keep the note of doubt out of the last words, despite her best efforts.

"I could do that," Emma said. "But then I'd have to go shopping and to lunch by myself, and we'd both miss out on making a new friend. Not to mention we'd have to listen to my husband and Ryan rake us over the coals when they found out I had left you alone, and that's just tiresome." She lowered her sunglasses to look Jana in the eye. "You don't really want to do that, do you?"

Jana gave a shaky laugh. "Well, when you put it that way."

"Terrific." Emma put the car in gear and headed out of the parking lot. Jana resisted the urge to look back at the officers swarmed around her car and instead sipped the coffee. It was hot and sweet—and maybe exactly what she needed.

"How's your head this morning?" Emma asked. "I heard you were knocked out."

"It doesn't hurt as much as it did last night." She sipped the coffee. "Thanks for the latte. Ryan made coffee, but…"

"But it was strong enough to put hair on your chest." Emma laughed. "Cop coffee. They're more interested in caffeine than taste. You'll get used to it."

"Oh, I…" Jana let her voice trail away, not sure what kind of answer to give.

"Have a muffin." Emma passed her the bag and a napkin. "Let me guess—part of you wants to protest that you're not going to stick around long enough to form an opinion about Ryan's coffee one way or another. But another part of you thinks the studly single cop is pretty darn interesting—am I right?"

Jana peeled the paper back from her muffin and pinched off a bite, then nodded. When she had woken up this morning to find herself alone in Ryan's bed, she'd been disappointed. The more time she spent with Ryan, the more her attraction for him grew. Their timing was lousy—any sensible person would tell her that getting involved with a man when her emotions were in such turmoil over Jenny's disappearance was a bad idea, but her heart wasn't paying attention to sense.

"Graham and I got together when some thug took a shot at me and Graham appointed himself my bodyguard," Emma said. She took a bite of muffin and chewed, cherry-pink lips curved in a half smile. "I thought he was the most insufferable, overbearing, bossy man I had ever met—and also the sexiest, smartest and most fascinating."

"Now isn't exactly the best time to start a relationship," Jana said.

"Honey, it is never the right time for a relationship with a cop," Emma said. "But don't let that stop you. For what it's worth, I think Ryan is definitely interested in you."

"What makes you say that?" There she went, blushing again.

"Are you kidding? He couldn't keep his eyes off you just now."

But maybe that was only because he thought she was going to lose it any minute. Certainly, the whole time she had known him she had been upset about one thing or the other—her sister or being attacked or having her car destroyed. Time to change the subject. "You said you're a reporter. Do you know Eric Patterson?"

Emma signaled for the turn onto the highway. "I know who he is," she said. "We've run into each other a couple of times, but we're not friends or anything."

"What's your impression of him?"

"You meet a lot of guys like him in my business—maybe in any business. He's ambitious. A little narcissistic. He has a reputation as something of a ladies' man."

Emma wouldn't have guessed that last one. "He does?"

"Well, he's the kind of smooth talker who seems to think every woman should fall under his spell." She shrugged. "That type never impresses me, but some women seem to go for it."

"He was engaged to my sister," Jana said.

"So I hear."

"But Jenny wasn't the type to fall for a

smooth operator. She liked more—I don't know—self-effacing guys. Easygoing, athletic maybe, but with a good sense of humor." She ran through the list of men Jenny had dated seriously—a singer/songwriter, a computer-technology major, a rodeo cowboy—none of them at all like Eric Patterson.

"Maybe your sister was attracted to Eric because he was so different from her usual type," Emma said. "Or maybe she was going through a phase where she was experimenting with different things. Some people do that in college. You know, they find religion or they become obsessed with a band or start reading philosophy or dressing like a 1950s pinup girl. It's part of growing up."

"Maybe. Jenny was into different things lately. She never said anything to me, but apparently she'd been reading a blog written by Daniel Metwater."

"Ah, our local prophet." Emma nodded. "Your sister wouldn't be the first young woman to fall under his spell."

Jana leaned forward. "What do you know about Metwater and his followers?" she asked. "They seem like some throwback hippie cult or something to me."

"They are that, in a way." Emma took another drink of coffee. "Metwater is actually a really interesting guy. He's the son of a wealthy industrialist. He and his brother inherited the family fortune, but the brother got into a lot of trouble, embezzling money from the family business. He ended up dead—supposedly murdered by the mob, though that was never proven. As far as I could determine, that case is still open. Anyway, supposedly the shock of his brother's death led Daniel to renounce his capitalist roots and turn to spiritual pursuits. He preaches a lot about living apart from society, being at one with nature, et cetera."

"Do you think he's sincere?" Jana asked.

"His followers have to sign over all their worldly possessions to him when they join his so-called Family," she said. "That doesn't sound like someone who's really committed to living a nonmaterialistic life. And for all he preaches peace, he's had a pretty antagonistic relationship with the Rangers."

"Do you think he had anything to do with the women who have been disappearing?" Jana asked.

"It doesn't matter what I think," Emma said. "But I can tell you the Rangers think there's a lot more going on out there at his camp than an innocent gathering of peace-loving nature worshippers."

RYAN WAS ON his way to Ranger headquarters when Simon called and asked him to pick up the mail. "It comes to a PO Box and the admin who's supposed to collect it forgot," Simon said. "Just flash your badge and they shouldn't give you any trouble about getting it."

Twenty minutes later, Ryan stepped into headquarters carrying a large plastic tub filled with letters and packages. "Simon, there's a thick envelope for you from the Chicago police department," he said.

"Great." Simon snagged the envelope and tore open the flap.

Ryan leaned over his shoulder to study the cheaply bound volume of what looked like police reports.

"It's a copy of the files the Chicago police had on Daniel Metwater and his brother." Simon tossed the thick book on the corner of his desk. "I got curious about what they thought might have happened."

"What did happen?" Ryan asked. This was the first he had heard of Metwater having a brother.

"The brother, David, was murdered," Simon said. "We had always heard local police suspected a mafia hit, but I wanted to see for sure."

"Not a bad idea." Ethan joined Ryan and the

others by Simon's desk. "Maybe you'll find something interesting." He turned to Ryan. "Anything for me?"

"Nope. And not for me, either." He turned toward Carmen. "I have a package for you, though." He hefted the large cardboard box. "From a Wilma Redhorse. Is that your sister?"

"My mother." She took the box and carried it to her desk.

"Your mother sends you packages at work?" Simon followed her to her desk.

"Did she send you cookies?" Ethan asked. "Because I'm getting kind of hungry."

"I don't know what's in here." She took a pair of scissors from her desk drawer and began snipping at the thick layers of packing tape all around the box. "And she sends them to me here because she's convinced that if I'm not home and the carrier leaves the box on the front porch, someone will steal it."

"It happens." Ryan sat on the corner of her desk. "Maybe it is cookies."

She snipped the last of the tape and pulled back the flaps on the box. Then she pulled out a large ball of tissue paper. "She sent you a soccer ball," Ethan said.

"That's a lot of paper," Randall said. "Maybe it's a crystal ball and she doesn't want it to get broken."

"Why would my mom have a crystal ball?" Carmen asked. She began unwinding the many layers of tissue paper, then stopped, a look of horror stealing over her face. "Oh, no."

"Oh, no what?" Ryan stood. Beneath her normally tanned complexion, Carmen had gone very white.

She shook her head and started to stuff the tissue wad back into the box, but Simon intercepted her. "You can't bring us this far, then just stop," he said. "We all want to know what your mom sent."

She pulled away from him, but reluctantly removed the rest of the paper and scowled at the item in her hand.

Simon stared. "Is it a crown?"

Ryan looked in the box. "There's a sash in here, too." He held it up and read the gold lettering across the red satin. "Miss Northern Ute."

Ryan looked at Carmen, who was very red now. "You were a beauty queen?"

"Don't sound so shocked." She snatched the sash from him and stuffed it and the crown back into the box. "Not another word," she said, and tucked the box under her arm and left the room.

"What's wrong with her?" Randall asked.

"If I were ever a beauty queen, I'd be proud of it."

"I can't tell you how grateful I am to live in a world where you are not a beauty queen," Simon said.

"Speaking of beauty queens, Andi Mattheson will be here any minute," Ethan said. "Marco and Michael are bringing her in for questioning."

"Call her Asteria if you want her to cooperate," Simon said. "Though I have my doubts we'll get anything out of her. Metwater has her thoroughly brainwashed." He turned to Graham. "I want to be in on the interview."

"Fine," Graham said. "But I want Ryan and Ethan there, too. They don't have the history with Metwater the rest of us do. She might let her guard down with them."

"Yes, sir," Ryan said. "And thanks again for sending your wife over to stay with Jana."

"I don't send Emma anywhere," the commander said. "She does what she wants and she didn't think Jana should be left alone right now. And, despite her glamour-girl looks, she knows how to take care of herself. Jana will be safe with her."

Maybe. But Ryan wouldn't rest until he caught whoever was terrorizing her and put a stop to it. He had to put those concerns aside, however, when Marco and Michael arrived, Andi/Asteria between them. The young woman wore a loose white gauze dress that flowed over her pregnant belly, and her blond hair was loose and hung almost to her waist. Only the coldness in her eyes when she looked at the officers belied her otherwise angelic appearance.

Marco and Michael led her to the conference room, and Ryan and Ethan followed them inside. The first two officers left and Ryan sat across from her. She had the kind of polished blond beauty that had kept her picture in the magazines, newspapers and on online gossip sites from the time she was a teenager. Though she had given up her designer gowns and expensive haircuts for peasant blouses and long, straight hair, she was still gorgeous, but Ryan thought there was something brittle about her beauty—push her too hard and she would crack open to reveal something ugly within.

Of course, that was exactly what the Rangers hoped to do today—to question Andi Mattheson until she cracked and gave them something that would link Daniel Metwater to the deaths of Alicia Mendoza and possibly two other women. "Thank you for coming in today to speak with us," Ryan began. He might as well get started, though Simon had yet to make an appearance.

"I didn't really have a choice, did I?" she said, fixing him with that cool gaze that made him feel about two feet tall.

"Can we get you anything before we begin?" Ethan asked. "Coffee or water?"

"No."

The door to the conference room opened and Simon stepped in. He handed Andi a bottle of water, then sat in the chair beside her, ignoring the other two officers. "Miss Matheson, you live with Daniel Metwater, is that correct?" he asked.

"My name is Asteria." She gave him a frosty look worthy of a star accustomed to dealing with impertinent paparazzi.

"All right, Asteria," Simon emphasized the name, his voice just short of a sneer. "You live with Daniel Metwater in his motor home."

"I do not," she said. "I have my own tent."

"But you spend a great deal of time with him," Simon said. "You've answered the door almost every time Rangers have visited Mr. Metwater in his motor home."

"I act as the Prophet's personal secretary," she said.

"His secretary," Simon repeated.

"Why shouldn't I? I have a degree from Brown. Where did you go to school, Officer?"

"Tulane."

This information surprised Ryan. Tulane University wasn't Ivy League, but it was certainly a prestigious university.

Simon's gaze never left Andi's face. He had a particularly intense expression at the best of times, eyes so dark they were almost black, boring into the object of his attention, as if daring the other person to blink first. "You and Daniel Metwater are close," he said.

"If you're asking if I'm sleeping with him, that is none of your business," she said.

"Fine." Simon looked away, his normally sallow complexion flushed.

Ryan decided it was time for him to step in. "As Mr. Metwater's personal secretary, you keep track of his schedule, is that correct?" he asked.

"I log any appointments he might have on his calendar," she said. "But I don't account for his movements every minute of the day. I'm his assistant, not his minder."

She's been coached, Ryan thought. Someone—Metwater or his lawyer—had told her not to admit to knowing Metwater's whereabouts around the times the three women disappeared. "Were you with Mr. Metwater on July 22?" Ryan asked.

"I have no idea," she said. "That was weeks ago."

"What about August tenth?" Simon asked. "That was only four days ago."

"I was probably with the Prophet. I spend most days with him."

Simon leaned toward her and she shifted, leaning away from him, and put one hand protectively over her pregnant belly, which swelled the front of her loose cotton dress. "Tell me about a day you didn't spend with Daniel Metwater," Simon said.

She frowned. "Which day?"

"Any day recently that you haven't spent with the Prophet," Simon said.

"I… I've spent every day with him for the last—well, for at least the last month," she said.

"Do you mean you've spent all of every day in Metwater's company for the past month?" Simon asked.

"Yes."

"You haven't left to—for example—go to a doctor's appointment?" Simon stared pointedly at her belly.

She rubbed her hands together. "I'm very healthy. I don't need to see a doctor."

"No problems with blurred vision? I noticed you keep rubbing your hands. Are they numb or tingling? Have you been thirsty more lately?"

"I'm fine." She pushed back her chair. "Why are you wasting my time like this?"

Simon put his hand out to stay her. "I only want to know why you haven't left the camp in the last month," he said. "Before that you would go into town with the other women to shop and do laundry. I've seen you there."

"Yes, but we thought it was best for me to stay closer to camp."

"Who is we?" Simon asked. "Was this your idea or Metwater's?"

"We decided together."

"Why? What prompted the decision?" Simon's voice was sharp.

Too sharp, Ryan thought. "We're only concerned for your well-being and that of your baby," he said, trying to de-escalate the situation.

Andi didn't even glance at him, her gaze fixed on Simon. "I don't need to go into town," she said. "I have everything I need at the camp, and I'm safe there."

"Why wouldn't you be safe in town?" Ryan asked, before Simon could speak.

Andi smoothed her dress over her belly, her

hand rubbing back and forth. "The Prophet offered to send one of his personal bodyguards with me if I wanted to go into town," she said. "But there's really nothing I need there."

"The other women don't have bodyguards," Simon said. "Why would you need one?"

She looked away, but not before Ryan caught the troubled expression in her eyes. "Did something happen to frighten you?" he asked, keeping his voice gentle.

"A man tried to grab me as I was coming out of the grocery store rather late at night," she said, her head down so that he couldn't see much of her face. "I screamed and kicked at him. I kicked him in the groin and when he doubled over, I ran."

"Why didn't you report this to the police?" Simon asked.

"Because we don't involve the police in our affairs." She raised her head and glared at him. "If you knew anything at all about us, you would know that. We're a family. We take care of our own."

"So your response to this attack was to simply stay home?" Simon asked.

"I stayed where I knew I would be safe."

"Did you get a look at the man who grabbed you?" Ryan asked.

"No. It was dark and he was behind me. I was terrified he was going to hurt my baby."

Ryan could hear the terror in her voice still. The method the man had used was so similar to that used by Jana's attacker it made the hair on the back of his neck stand up. "What grocery store was this?" he asked.

"The City Market on the north side of town," she said. "I parked around by the Dumpsters because I dropped off some of our trash there."

The store was only a couple of miles from Jenny Lassiter's apartment, where Jana had been attacked, but it still might be only coincidence. "Have any of the other women in the Family been attacked?" Ryan asked.

"No." She swallowed. "The man knew me. He called me by name."

"He called you Andi?" Simon asked.

"No, he called me by my name now. He called me Asteria." She pressed her hands over her eyes, as if trying to shut out whatever visions were replaying in her head. "He said he had been watching me and he knew I was perfect for his next victim."

Simon grabbed her wrist and gently lowered her hand. "You're sure those were his words?" he asked. "His next victim?"

She nodded. "I was so terrified. And when

I heard about those other women going missing, I wondered…" Her voice trailed away and she shook her head.

"What did you wonder?" Ryan prompted.

"I wondered if I would have died that night if I hadn't gotten away," she said. "Would I have ended up buried by the side of the road like Alicia Mendoza?"

"WHERE ARE WE HEADED?" Jana asked, after she and Emma had finished their coffee and muffins and Emma turned the car back toward town.

"Have you been to The Boardwalk since you've been in town?" Emma asked.

"I haven't been much of anywhere lately," Jana said.

"Of course you haven't. So you definitely need a break. Do you like antiques?"

"Sure."

"How about rustic art, jewelry and old signs?"

Jana laughed. "Jewelry, yes. I don't know anything about the other two."

"The Boardwalk is a collection of antiques and junk shops on the south end of town," Emma said. "I'm in the process of redecorating the house Graham was living in when we married, giving it a more local vibe, if you will. I'm always on the lookout for interesting things to add to my collection. So if you'll indulge me…"

"It sounds perfect," Jana said. A few hours focused on rusting farm implements and old furniture was just the distraction she needed. "But could we swing by my motel first? I meant to call them this morning and forgot. I still need to check out."

"No problem. And when we're done shopping, I know a great place for lunch."

Ten minutes later, Emma pulled the convertible beneath the portico for the Columbine Inn. She followed Jana inside. "Not that I think you really need a bodyguard," she said, linking her arm with Jana's. "But let's humor Ryan. It's kind of sexy sometimes when a guy goes all protective on you, don't you think?"

Ryan Spencer was sexy pretty much all the time, Jana thought. But maybe she was a tiny bit prejudiced. What was it about the man that got to her so?

The desk clerk greeted Jana by name and accepted her key card. "We hope you enjoyed your stay with us," she said.

Except for the part about someone trying to break into my room, Jana thought. Then again, Ryan would have already notified them about that. "It was fine," she said.

She accepted the receipt the clerk handed her and turned to go. She and Emma were almost to the door when a familiar voice hailed them. "You are just the woman I've been looking for!"

Eric Patterson jogged up to them, out of breath. "Are you okay?" he asked.

"I'm fine." She knew he was just being nice, but something about him always rubbed her the wrong way.

"I heard about what happened," he said, taking her hand. "You could have been killed."

Thanks for pointing that out, she thought. "How did you hear about it?" she asked, pulling her hand away.

"I read the police report. And your Jeep, too." He shook his head. "I wouldn't recommend playing the lottery if I were you," he said. "You've had a run of really bad luck."

"I think being hit over the head and having your car destroyed qualify as more than bad luck," Emma said.

"Hello, Emma," Eric said, his manner more subdued.

"Hello, Eric. You really do get around, don't you?"

"What do you mean?"

"Well, I understand you were with Daniel Metwater when the Rangers arrested him yesterday and you still had time to read the police blotter this morning. When do you sleep?"

His expression grew stormy. "I was at the local cop shop this morning checking on the disposition of Daniel Metwater's case and asked a cop I know there if anything interesting had happened overnight. That's what makes me a good reporter. I'm always on the lookout for my next scoop."

"What is the disposition of Daniel Metwater's case?" Jana asked.

"He was released on bail this morning," Eric said.

"Really?" Emma asked.

"Would I lie?" He grinned. "And I've got a statement from his lawyer that he doesn't expect the grand jury to indict. The Rangers don't have enough evidence linking him to that woman's murder."

"But Ryan said they had evidence," Jana said.

"They have a shirt," Eric said. "It's not enough. But you can believe the Rangers will be keeping a very close eye on him. If he strikes again, they'll be on him like that." He snapped his fingers.

"So you think he's guilty?" Emma asked.

"Oh yeah," Eric said. "I mean look at the

guy—handsome, smooth talker, irresistible to women—we're talking Ted Bundy all over again."

Jana felt sick to her stomach. "So you think he not only killed Alicia Mendoza, but Lucia Raton and Jenny, too?"

"I'm hoping I'm wrong, but we have to prepare ourselves for the worst." He took her hand again, and this time she didn't pull away. She needed every bit of her strength to remain standing against the fear and grief that rocked her. "You need to be careful yourself," he said.

"Why is that?" she asked.

"Because you don't want whoever attacked you last night to try again." He leaned forward and kissed her cheek, his voice gentle. "I may have lost Jenny, but I don't want to lose you, too."

Chapter Eleven

"Andi Mattheson swears the man who attacked her was not Daniel Metwater." Simon wrote this information on the whiteboard in the conference room, the marker squeaking above the buzz of the fluorescent lights. Marco and Michael had returned Andi to the Family's camp and the Rangers had convened to review the case.

"Daniel Metwater was in the Montrose jail when Jana and her car were attacked," Ryan said.

"The lab confirms that the material used to strangle Alicia Mendoza came from the shirt we found in Daniel Metwater's closet," Ethan said. "We're still waiting on the DNA results to prove that Metwater wore the shirt, but it matches the other shirts in his closet."

"But we don't have anything to place him

away from his camp when Alicia, Lucia or Jenny went missing," Graham said.

"We've got half-a-dozen witnesses or more who will swear Metwater never left camp during those time periods," Marco added.

"We only have Andi's word that she was attacked," Graham said. "She could be making up the story to bolster Metwater's case."

"Maybe," Ryan agreed. "But she sounded genuinely terrified to me."

"Terrified of Metwater, maybe," Simon said. "He's been practically holding her prisoner."

"And we know Jana isn't making up her story," Ryan said. "And Metwater was definitely with us at that time."

"Maybe he had one of his disciples carry out the attack," Marco said.

"Maybe," Graham said. "The problem with our case is we have too many maybes."

"What if we're looking at this wrong?" Ethan said. "What if Metwater isn't the killer and by focusing on him, we're letting the real culprit go free?"

"Who else is a likely suspect?" Graham asked.

"There's the mysterious 'Easy.'" Ethan tapped his pen on the notebook in front of him. "When the women in Metwater's camp were interviewed shortly after Lucia Raton went missing, they mentioned seeing her with someone named 'Easy.' Now when we ask about him, everyone denies having seen him."

"The waitress at the café by the lake mentioned seeing Lucia having coffee with a man," Ethan said. "That was the last time anyone saw her. Maybe it was this 'Easy' fellow."

"That's all we've got?" Ryan asked. "Easy?"

"That's what the people in camp called him," Marco said. "The woman who first gave us the information said he wasn't a member of the Family, but he ran errands for Metwater sometimes."

"So we see if we can find out more about Easy," Graham said. "Circulate his description again, see if we get any hits."

"That still leaves the shirt," Ryan said. "How do you explain it?"

"Someone could have planted it to implicate Metwater," Ethan said.

Graham nodded. "Who has access to Metwater's closet?"

"Probably almost any of his followers," Simon said.

Marco sat back, arms across his chest. "So what do we do now? Go back to the camp and start questioning everyone?"

"We haven't gotten anywhere doing that so far," Graham said.

"I think we should lean on Eric Patterson," Ryan said.

The others turned toward him. "Why Patterson?" Marco asked.

Ryan sat up straighter. "Lean on him was probably a poor choice of words. I think we should ask him for his help. He's doing this newspaper story on Metwater—he has access to the camp and seems to be on good terms with everyone there. Maybe he's learned something that will help us."

"Asking the press for help is asking for trouble," Simon said.

"I used to feel that way," Graham said. "Before I married a reporter." He nodded to Ryan. "Approach Patterson. See if he's got anything for us." He turned back to the whiteboard. "One problem is that we don't know for sure that these cases are connected. We've got three missing women—one we know is dead—and two assaults. They're all young women and they all happened in this general area, but, beyond that, we don't have any link."

"They all knew the killer," Ethan said.

"Maybe," Simon said. "But maybe they were random targets. Maybe the only link is that the killer knew them."

"Or maybe there isn't a link," Marco said.

"They're unrelated cases and we're wasting our time trying to connect them."

"Then find something to either prove or disprove the connection," Graham said.

"It might help if we knew what happened to the two missing women," Ethan said.

"Maybe looking at what we know about Alicia's death can help us," Graham said. He moved to the whiteboard and took the marker from Simon. "So what do we know?"

"She was killed soon after she disappeared," Ethan said. "Within hours."

"She was strangled," Ryan said. "And the body buried in a shallow grave on the side of the highway, in an area where there had been recent road construction."

"The killer was in a hurry," Simon said. "He had a car or truck or van, pulled over and dumped the body."

"He was lazy," Marco said. "He didn't want to work hard digging a grave, so he looked for a place where the ground was already disturbed."

"Maybe that's a pattern," Simon said. "We look for other shallow graves in disturbed ground and/or near roads. He wants to get in and out quickly, with as little trouble as possible."

Ryan made a note of this on his tablet.

"Why kill an immigrant in the middle of no-where?" he asked. "She hadn't been in the country long enough for him to stalk her, and she wasn't anywhere where very many people would have seen her."

"Metwater would have seen her if she came to his camp," Simon said. "If she got lost and went looking for help."

"Or one of his men would have," Ethan said.

"Who else?" Graham asked.

Ryan sat up straight, heart pounding. "One of the archaeologists. Their site was near there. They would have known about Jenny Lassiter, too." Why hadn't they thought of that before? They had been so focused on Daniel Metwater they might have overlooked the real killer.

"Go back and ask questions there," Graham said. "Find out if any of the men working at the dig site knew Lucia Raton. And run some backgrounds. Find out if any of them have priors for sexual assault, domestic violence, stalking—anything that raises flags."

"I'll take the archaeologists," Ethan said.

"I'll go with you," Ryan said. "I can talk to Eric Patterson when we're done at the dig site."

"Simon, you and Marco run down every-thing you can on Easy." Graham set aside the marker and stood back to study the whiteboard. "We're going to get this guy. We have to do it before he strikes again."

JANA ALL BUT ran to Emma's car and was already buckled into her seat when Emma joined her. "Let's get out of here," Jana said. She glanced toward the motel lobby, where she could just see Eric standing inside the door.

"On our way." Emma started the engine. "Are you okay?"

"Just a little creeped out." Jana shuddered. "What did Eric mean, saying he didn't want to lose me? He never had me."

"Maybe he's one of those overly friendly guys—they don't get the concept of boundaries. Or maybe he's doing it on purpose because he can see it freaks you out."

"I am officially freaked-out." She rubbed her hands up and down her arms. "And I feel like I need a shower." She turned to Emma. "Do you think I'm overreacting?"

"No." She turned onto the highway. "But instead of a shower, why don't we try a little retail therapy to help you feel better?"

Jana would have thought she wasn't in the mood for shopping, but Emma's relentless good humor pulled her out of her funk. The two women explored every inch of the half-dozen shops in the collection of eclectic buildings beside the highway. Emma purchased an old metal gas-station sign that promised You Can Trust Your Car to the Man Who Wears the Star.

"It's perfect for Graham's birthday," she said. "We can hang it on the back deck, by the barbecue grill."

In a boutique Jana bought a bracelet made of wire-wrapped glass beads, and a key fob of hammered brass and leather. "Ooh, that looks nice," Emma said, leaning over Jana's shoulder to admire the piece. "Who's it for?"

Jana pretended to search for something in her purse. "I thought, maybe, when this is all over, I'd give it to Ryan to thank him for all the help he's given me," she said.

"You mean, like a going-away gift?" Emma asked.

"I do have a job and home in Denver to go back to."

"We have jobs and homes in Montrose, too," Emma said, her tone teasing. "If, you know, you decide to stay for some reason."

"I can't decide anything until I know what's happened to Jenny," Jana said. If it turned out her sister was dead, could she bear to stay in the town where she had died?

After lunch at a tea shop and more shopping, the women headed back to Ryan's duplex in the late afternoon. "Look who's home," Emma said as they turned the corner. Ryan's cruiser sat in the driveway. Emma parked behind it and as the women climbed out of the car, the front door opened.

"I was getting ready to call and check in with you," Ryan said, stepping onto the front porch.

"We went shopping, had lunch and did more shopping," Emma said. She hugged Jana. "I hope I see you again."

"I hope so. And thanks for everything."

Emma waved away the thanks. "I didn't do anything."

"But you did." Jana squeezed her hand. "You listened, and you did your best to distract me. That means a lot."

"Good luck," Emma said. "I hope you find your sister soon." She waved and headed back to her car. Jana waited until she'd left, then followed Ryan into the house.

"I'm making dinner," he said. "I hope you like grilled chicken."

"It sounds good." She dropped her purse and her packages on the end of the sofa and followed him into the kitchen. He had changed out of his uniform and wore jeans and an Old 97's T-shirt, his feet bare. This more laid-back version of Ryan was even more appealing than the cop in uniform who had first captured her attention.

"Did you have a good time today?" he asked.

"Emma was a lot of fun." She leaned back against the counter and he opened a cabinet and began pulling out bottles of spices. "I'm still trying to picture her married to your commander. He seems so severe and she's anything but."

"He's not severe around her. Maybe that's the secret." He glanced back at her. "How's your head?"

"It's not hurting anymore." She touched the lump on the back of her head and winced. "At least not much. I went by and checked out of my motel."

"Good. I meant to remind you this morning and forgot." He began measuring different spices into a bowl.

"A kind of strange thing happened while I was there."

He set down the measuring spoons and turned to face her, giving her his full attention. "What was that?"

"Eric Patterson was there—in the motel lobby. He said he'd been looking for me. He told me Daniel Metwater was released on bail."

"Yes."

"He also told me Metwater's lawyer thinks you don't have enough evidence to get the grand jury to indict him."

"At this point, he may be right. Without a stronger case, we have to remain open to the idea that Metwater may not be the man responsible for these crimes. Or maybe not all of them. It could be that he attacked Alicia Mendoza, but not the other women. We're expanding our investigation to look at other suspects."

"What other suspects?"

"I can't tell you that." His voice was gentle but firm.

Of course he couldn't. She gripped the edge of the counter and looked down at her shoes. "Eric knew what had happened to me, and to my Jeep," she said. "He said a police officer friend of his told him."

"Is that what has you so upset? The prospect of Daniel Metwater out of jail?" He closed the gap between them and rested his hands on her shoulders. "I promise you'll be safe here with me."

She nodded. "I feel safe with you. And that isn't what upset me—or at least not the main thing."

He squeezed her shoulders gently. "What is it, then?"

She raised her head to look into his eyes. The tenderness and concern she found there steadied her. "When Eric left, he kissed my cheek and told me to be careful. He said he had already lost Jenny, and he didn't want to lose me, too. The way he said it, as if I really meant something to him, creeped me out. I hardly know the man. I don't even like him."

"He rubs me the wrong way, too," Ryan said. "But maybe he really does care about you, as his fiancée's sister. You're a link for him to her."

"Maybe. Emma said he has a reputation as a ladies' man. The smooth-operator type."

"I can see that."

"But I can't see Jenny with a man like him. It's so frustrating."

"It is. And it's frustrating not to know what happened to your sister." He gave her shoulders a final squeeze and turned back to his cooking. "We're working every angle we can think of, believe me."

"What did you do today?" she asked as he mixed the seasonings.

"I pulled at threads to see where they would lead." He took a plate of chicken breasts from the refrigerator.

"And where did they lead?"

"Nowhere so far." He sprinkled the seasoning mixture over the chicken. "But tomorrow is a new day and we have some new leads to follow. Maybe that will lead us somewhere constructive. Right now, let's grill this chicken so we can eat."

She followed him onto the back deck and sat in a lounge chair while he grilled the chicken, the scent of cooking meat mingling with the perfume of flowers that grew along the fence around the backyard. It was such a relaxing, domestic scene. Jana felt guilty for enjoying it so much while her sister was missing. Shouldn't she be doing something to try to find her? But what?

Jana would have said she wasn't hungry, but she ate every bite of the grilled chicken and vegetables Ryan prepared, accompanied by a glass of crisp white wine. "You're spoiling me, waiting on me like this," she said when her plate was empty.

"You've had a rough time of it. You deserve a little pampering." His eyes met hers across the table and she felt warmed through. The tenderness she had seen earlier was still there, but heightened by a wanting that echoed her own desire. Last night her injury and shock had been an unacknowledged barrier between them, but now she had no such shield to hide behind. Nor did she want to hide.

She slipped off her shoes and propped one foot on his knee. His hand caressed her instep, then began massaging her toes. She let out a low moan. "I'll give you an hour and forty-five minutes to stop that."

He continued massaging, working his way up her calf to her knee, leaning forward to reach her thigh. He stilled, eyes locked to hers. "Why are you stopping?" she asked.

"I'm not sure how far you want this to go."

She could be coy and pretend she didn't know what he was talking about, but she was past playing those kinds of games, amusing as they could be. She slid from his grasp, stood and walked around the table to him.

He leaned back, his expression guarded, until she took his chin in her hand and kissed him. "Why don't we see how it feels to go a little further?" she asked.

Ryan pulled Jana into his lap and kissed her, a long, drugging kiss that started at her lips and reverberated through her whole body, leaving her flushed and tingling and wanting more. "I'm thinking we should take it a lot further," she said, and slid her hand under his T-shirt, the warm muscles of his stomach trembling at her touch.

"Are you sure?" he asked, his voice husky.

"Right now, it's the only thing I *am* sure of." She kissed his throat, sweeping her tongue across his pulse. "I want to be with you."

Chapter Twelve

Ryan stood and led Jana toward the bedroom. Standing beside the bed, they undressed each other slowly, pausing often to kiss a bare shoulder or run a hand across a newly exposed expanse of skin. Anticipation trembled between them, both eager for completion but determined to savor the moment, to indulge in the sweet torture of prolonging the experience as much as possible.

When they were both naked, they lay side by side on the bed, continuing their exploration of each other's bodies. She reveled in the feel of him, and in the sensations he created in her. To find such joy in the midst of her sorrow over Jenny moved her almost to tears, but she pushed them away. Tonight was a gift, and she intended to wring every bit of pleasure from it.

He began kissing his way down her torso,

lingering over first one breast and then the other until she was panting and arching toward him. He moved farther down, pressing a hand to her belly, steadying her, and the tension within her coiled even tighter. When his lips found her sex she cried out, not in pain but in pleasure, and felt him smile against her.

He rose on his knees, opened the drawer in the bedside table and took out a condom packet. After he had sheathed himself, she reached for him, no longer content to wait. She welcomed him into her, wrapping her body around his and moving with him in a rhythm that was both familiar and brand-new. He caressed her hips, guiding her, then slid one hand down between them to stroke her, his sure touch bringing her quickly over the edge.

She gripped him ever tighter as he reached his own climax, and she pressed her forehead to his shoulder, grounded by the feel of muscle and bone. So many relationships in her life had been built on what she and her partner could give to each other or do for each other. When had she ever been so content to simply be with a man? When had the mere fact of his presence meant so much to her?

RYAN HAD NO need to lie awake that night. He slept with Jana's body pressed to his and woke early to make love to her again. Getting involved with the sister of a crime victim complicated matters—that went without saying. But in his experience every relationship involved negotiating complications of one kind or another. He couldn't be sorry something good had come out of one of the most perplexing cases of his career.

"I need to go back out to the dig site this morning to talk to Jeremy Eddleston," he said as he and Jana finished a breakfast of coffee and waffles. "I stopped by there yesterday afternoon, but he wasn't around. One of his workers said he would be back this morning."

"Why are you questioning Eddleston again?" she asked. Her hair curled around her face, still damp from her shower, and she was no longer deathly pale, her cheeks warmed by a pink flush that he liked to think he could take credit for.

"We just had a few things we needed to clear up. I'd like you to come with me. You can wait in the cruiser while I talk to Eddleston, then we'll swing by Ranger headquarters."

"I should see about renting a car today," she said. "You don't have to babysit me."

"Don't think of it as babysitting." He rinsed his coffee cup and set it on the drain board.

"Think of it as keeping myself from being distracted worrying about you."

"You can't keep me with you twenty-four hours a day forever," she said. "What if it takes weeks to solve this case? What if you never find out who attacked me?"

She was right, of course. It wasn't practical or fair to her to keep her under lock and key for long. "Stay with me today," he said. "We'll figure something out."

"Fair enough." She pushed back her chair and stood. "Let me grab my laptop so I can get some work done while you're on the job."

When Ryan and Jana arrived at the dig site an hour later, he was surprised to see a rental moving truck parked with the other vehicles. "Are they delivering something or hauling it away?" Jana asked.

"That's something I'll find out." He left her in the car and walked out to the base of the mesa, where he found Jeremy Eddleston surrounded by wooden packing crates.

"Good morning, Professor," Ryan said.

Eddleston looked up. "What are you doing here?" he asked. "As you can see, I'm very busy."

"Moving?" Ryan studied the stenciling on the box nearest him. Department of Archaeology, Colorado Mesa University.

"We're shutting down the site for the season and sending our equipment and the artifacts we've recovered back to the university, where they will be cataloged, cleaned and studied."

"I won't keep you," Ryan said. He took out his phone and pulled up the picture of Alicia Mendoza. "Do you know this woman?"

Eddleston leaned forward to squint at the image on the phone screen. "No," he said, and straightened.

"You're sure you haven't seen her around here, maybe near here?"

Eddleston shook his head. "I would particularly remember anyone trespassing on the dig site," he said. "We do get the occasional hiker or nosy tourist coming around and I quickly send them on their way." He lowered his sunglasses and peered over the top of them at Ryan. "I shouldn't have to tell you that antiquities theft is a serious crime—and a particular problem in remote sites like this one."

It was true that the Rangers had dealt with a case involving important Native American artifacts stolen from federal lands only last summer. "What about this woman?" Ryan scrolled to the photo of Lucia Raton.

Eddleston removed his sunglasses and studied the photo. "She looks familiar," he said. "Who is she?"

"She's another young woman who went missing in this area, a couple of weeks before Jenny Lassiter disappeared."

Eddleston replaced the sunglasses. "Then I must have seen her on the news."

Ryan pocketed his phone once more. "Can you tell me anything more about the day Jenny disappeared?" he asked.

"I've told you everything I know," Eddleston said.

"Maybe we should go over it again, in case you left anything out," Ryan said. "What was her mood that morning? Had the two of you argued?"

"Her mood was the same as always. Jenny was a normally cheerful person. We didn't argue. We didn't have anything to argue about."

"She wasn't upset you had decided to dump her to get back together with your wife?"

"I already told you, Jenny understood my decision. We were both adults, not two jealous kids."

"Adults have feelings. It wouldn't be unreasonable for her to feel hurt that you chose your wife over her."

"She wasn't upset." He slammed his hand down on one of the crates. "I don't have any more time to talk with you. Goodbye." He turned his back and strode toward the shade canopies, where a trio of students were boxing up more artifacts.

Ryan returned to the cruiser, frustration chafing at him. He slid into the driver's seat and slammed the door behind him. Jana looked up from her laptop. "What's wrong?" she asked.

"This case." He shoved the key into the ignition and started the engine. "We're not getting anywhere."

"I know you're trying," Jana said. "And I appreciate that. I hope the other families do, too."

"The problem is we don't have enough information. Which is why we have to keep digging."

He headed back to the highway but turned away from town. "Where are we going now?" Jana asked.

"I thought we might have a cup of coffee."

She gave him a puzzled look. "All right."

The Lakeside Café sported a vintage neon sign by the road and a carved wooden trout over the door, the once-bright pink-and-green paint on the fish faded by years of sun and wind. A cowbell hung on the back of the door and jangled when Ryan pushed it open. A curly-haired blonde with prominent front teeth looked up from behind the cash register. "Have a seat anywhere," she said.

Ryan led the way to a booth to the left of the door. The red leatherette seats sported several silver duct-tape repairs, and a plastic-coated placard on the Formica tabletop advertised the Friday night all-you-can-eat catfish. "You folks need menus?" The blonde approached their table.

"Just coffee for me," Ryan said. He looked across the table at Jana.

"Coffee for me, too," she said. "With cream."

"Do you want some pie with that?" the waitress asked. "We've got peach and cherry."

"It sounds wonderful, but I'll pass," Jana said.

"Thanks, but I'll pass, too," Ryan said.

"Is there a particular reason we stopped here?" Jana asked when they were alone again.

"This is the last place Lucia Raton was seen alive before she died," he said. "She was with a man we haven't been able to identify yet."

The waitress returned with two mugs, a cream pitcher and a coffeepot. "Sweetener is there by the salt and pepper," she said as she filled the mugs.

"Not very busy this time of afternoon," Ryan said as he accepted his cup.

"We'll pick up for dinner," she said. "All

the fishermen will come off the lake and be hungry." She laughed. "Usually for anything besides fish."

"Have you worked here long?" Ryan asked.

"Ten years." She looked around the room, with its battered booths and mismatched chairs. "I can hardly believe it. Who would want to hang around this place that long?"

Ryan laid his credentials open on the table. "Mind if I ask you a few questions?"

She lowered herself to the edge of the seat beside Jana. "I don't know if I have any answers, but go ahead."

He pulled up Lucia's picture on his phone and checked the waitress's name tag. "Mary, do you remember seeing this young woman in here?"

She looked at the photo and nodded. "She's the girl who disappeared a few weeks back. I remember the sheriff's department had someone in here asking about her. I saw her, with a guy who was maybe a little bit older than her. They stopped in for coffee, like you two."

"Would you recognize the man if you saw him again?" he asked.

"I think so. I have a pretty good memory for faces." She chuckled. "Don't ask me to remember any names, though."

He scrolled to another photo, Jeremy Eddleston's university ID image. "Was this the man with Lucia that afternoon?"

Mary leaned forward to study the image, then shook her head. "That wasn't him. He's too old, and I'd remember that pockmarked face. This was a younger guy. He wore a ball cap and sunglasses, but I still think I'd recognize him. At the time I thought maybe he was her older brother. He acted kind of, I don't know, protective of her. She had been crying, I could tell, and he seemed to be trying to comfort her."

Ryan scrolled to a photo of Daniel Metwater. "Was it this man?" he asked.

Mary checked the photo and shook her head again. "I know him. He's that preacher guy who was in the paper. Here, I'll show you." She jumped up and hurried to the cash register and returned with that day's issue of the *Montrose Daily Press*. She pointed to a picture of Daniel Metwater below the fold on the front page, accompanying an article with the headline A Voice in the Wilderness—Prophet Leads His Followers on Local Pilgrimage. The byline was Eric Patterson.

"He's a good-looking young fellow," Mary said. "So I would remember if he'd been in here, but he hasn't been."

"Have you seen the man who was with Lucia in here since that day?" Ryan asked.

"No." The bell on the door jangled and two men entered, fishermen judging by the canvas vests and caps they wore. "I'm sorry I wasn't more help to you," Mary said, and hurried to greet the newcomers.

Jana sipped her coffee and studied him across the table. "What?" Ryan asked after a moment.

"I'm debating whether or not to ask you if Jeremy Eddleston is a suspect in my sister's disappearance and the murder of those other women."

"Officially, Daniel Metwater is our only named suspect." He sipped his coffee.

"But you're not so sure he did it," she said.

"Let's just say I like to be thorough in my investigation."

His pulled out his wallet to pay their tab and his phone rang. "You need to get out to the old logging site on Red Creek Road," Randall Knightbridge said as soon as Ryan answered. "Some hikers have found another body."

Chapter Thirteen

Jana knew something was wrong when Ryan went rigid. The knuckles of the hand that gripped the phone turned white. "I'm on my way," he said, and ended the call. He dropped the phone into the console and shifted the cruiser out of Park.

"What is it?" she asked as he sped onto the highway.

"I have to drop you off at my place," he said. "Wait for me there."

"If there's an emergency, why not take me with you?" she asked. "I can stay in the car like I did this morning."

He shook his head. "You can't."

"Why not? It's a waste of time—not to mention gas—to drive me all the way back to your place if your business is in the park."

He said nothing, his jaw clenched.

"Ryan, tell me what's wrong," she said. "Don't shut me out."

He glanced at her before fixing his eyes once more on the road. "They've found another body," he said.

Her heart lurched, as if someone had reached out and squeezed her chest. She gripped the armrest and tried to force herself to breathe normally. "Can they tell—?"

"I don't know who it is," he said. "But you see why you can't be there."

"In case it's Jenny." She said the last word on a sob and tried to swallow down the emotion. *Keep it together*, she commanded herself. "If it is her, you'll have to tell me sooner rather than later," she said. "You might even need me to identify her." The thought made her stomach lurch.

"No," he said. "We don't ask family members to identify the body at the scene."

"Thank you," she said, her voice scarcely above a whisper. She breathed deeply through her nose, fighting for calm. "I can go with you. I can stay in the car. I promise not to interfere or get hysterical."

"Not a good idea," he said.

"It isn't a good idea to delay any longer than necessary," she said. "And what am I supposed to do at your place while you're gone? Do you think I won't go crazy wondering what is going on? And do you think I really want to be alone when you call to tell me what you've found?"

He said nothing, but stomped on the brakes and swung the cruiser around to face the other direction. "You'll stay in the vehicle and you won't say a word," he said. "You'll pretend you aren't there."

"I will," she agreed, relief flooding her, along with a new fear. What if she had lied and she wasn't able to keep it together, especially if the body did turn out to be Jenny? *Don't think that*, she reminded herself. *Don't borrow trouble.*

The cruiser sped down the highway, wind whipping up choppy waves on the surface of the lake to her right. Sun sparkled on the water and small fishing boats bobbed in the distance like children's bathtub toys. Ryan braked and turned the cruiser onto a dirt road that led away from the lake, up a steep grade into a thick growth of forest that contrasted sharply with the barren land closer to the water. The temperature felt twenty degrees cooler and the scent of pine came in through the air vents.

They bumped along for several miles, the woods growing thinner as they climbed, giving way to areas full of jutting stumps and scattered limbs. Jana spotted a trio of vehicles parked ahead: a faded red Jeep, a mint-green Forest Service truck and a black county sheriff's SUV. Ryan pulled in behind the SUV. Without a word, he climbed out and strode toward the three men and one woman standing beside the vehicles.

Jana studied the group. She decided the woman, and the one man not in uniform, must be hikers. They had probably found the body and called it in. They would have had to hike to the road to make the call, then maybe the sheriff or Forest Service ranger had given them a ride back up here so they could point out their find. They were young—early twenties, she guessed. Not much older than Jenny. The woman looked as if she had been crying. The man stood with one arm around her shoulder and nodded solemnly as Ryan spoke.

Then Ryan and the other officers turned away and started walking up the hill, leaving the couple alone. The man looked over at Jana, then walked toward her, the young woman at his side. Jana opened the door of the cruiser as they approached. "Hello," she said.

"Are you a cop, too?" the young man asked, with the hint of a Southern drawl.

"No," she said. She knew Ryan expected her to pretend to be invisible and not say anything, but she wasn't going to pass up this chance to learn information he probably wouldn't tell her. "Are you the ones who called in the… the find?" She couldn't bring herself to say "body." Further proof, if any was needed, that she would have made a lousy law-enforcement officer.

The girl nodded. "We were climbing over some fallen limbs, trying to find the trail, and I tripped and fell." She shuddered and chafed her hands up and down her arms. "I landed right on top of it."

The young man pulled her close. "It's okay, Rennie," he said. He looked back at Jana. "I thought it was an animal at first—you know, a deer or something. But then I saw the skull. It had long hair. And I knew it was a person."

"What color was the hair?" Jana asked. She had to force out the words and held her breath, anticipating the answer.

"Dark," the man said. "Though it was hard to tell much. I mean, it looked like it had been up here awhile and animals…" His voice trailed away. "Well, you know."

She closed her eyes and let out a long breath. Jenny's hair was blond. Surely this corpse could not be hers.

"We had to hike all the way to the road to get enough signal to call nine-one-one," the woman said. "Then we waited forever for someone to get here. I told Brian we should just leave once we'd made the call, but he said that wouldn't be right, and the cops would just trace us by our phone anyway. Can they really do that?"

"I don't know," she said. "But thank you for waiting. And for calling it in."

The sound of tires on gravel drew their attention and a second Ranger cruiser pulled in behind Ryan's. Officers Simon Woolridge and Ethan Reynolds got out and walked over to Jana and the young couple. "What are you doing here?" Simon asked Jana.

"I was with Ryan when he got the call," she said. "It was quicker to come straight here instead of dropping me off somewhere."

Simon grunted and headed up the hill, Ethan following. Halfway up, they met Ryan and the other two men making their way down. The men stopped and talked, and Simon handed Ryan a printout of some kind. Ryan scanned it, then looked down toward the cruiser.

He frowned when he saw the crowd gathered around his vehicle and began walking faster, quickly outpacing the other two. "Was I right?" Brian asked. "Is it a person?"

Ryan glanced at Jana. "We should talk somewhere else," he said.

"You can talk in front of me," she said. "I think I have a right to know."

Ryan studied the dirt between his feet. "You were right—the body is human. A female, shallow grave, maybe even just dumped in the ruts from the logging equipment they had up here in the spring. Looks like she's been up here awhile—maybe a few weeks, maybe longer."

"Any identifying clothing or jewelry?" Ethan asked.

"Dark hair," Ryan said. "Some animal depredation, but the clothes we found nearby were a denim skirt and jacket."

"That fits the description for Lucia Raton," Ethan said.

Ryan glanced at Jana. "Yeah, it does. We'll know more when we get the autopsy."

"Any idea how she was killed?" Simon asked.

Ryan shook his head. "We'll have to wait for the postmortem for that." He held up the phone. "I got some preliminary shots, but we'll want to get a forensics team up here, along with the coroner. I'll drive down and make the calls while you secure the scene." He moved around to the driver's side of the cruiser.

Jana didn't say anything until they reached the highway once more and Ryan had made his calls. Finally, he replaced the phone in his pocket and glanced at her. "Are you all right?" he asked.

She nodded. "Part of me is so relieved it wasn't Jenny," she said. "Does that make me a horrible person?"

"It makes you human." He pulled the cruiser back onto the highway and headed toward Montrose. "I'm taking you back to my place."

"All right." She knew he had work to do, even though the prospect of spending the evening alone with her doubts and worries troubled her. "I'm really glad that wasn't Jenny's body back there, but I'm frustrated that we still don't know what's happened to her," she said.

"We can't be sure Alicia's and Lucia's deaths are related," Ryan said. "Or if your sister's disappearance is part of this case."

"But you can't rule out a connection, either," Jana said.

He nodded. "We have to look at all the angles."

"What happens now?" she asked.

"The coroner will examine the body to determine cause of death, and we'll try to confirm the identity. If it is Lucia, we'll look for anything about her death that matches Alicia's murder. Sometimes patterns are clues about the murderer."

"Have you found any patterns so far?"

He glanced at her. "Jana, there are things you don't need to know."

She looked away. "Why do you get to decide what I do and don't need to know? We're talking about my only sister."

"The more people who know about evidence, the more likely it is to become compromised. And what are you going to do with the information anyway, but worry over it, trying to make connections where there aren't any?"

"How do you know there aren't any connections? Maybe I'll see something you don't."

"Or maybe there comes a time when you need to get on with your life and let us worry about solving the crime."

She felt the sting of his words as if he had slapped her. "Are you saying I need to go back to Denver and pretend none of this has happened?" *That you and I never happened?*

He slid his hands up and down the steering wheel. "When I came walking down that hill and saw you seated in the cruiser talking to that couple, all I could think was that you didn't belong there. You had no place at a crime scene and it wasn't right for me to bring you there."

"I wanted you to bring me there," she said. "I hate sitting around being helpless. I want to be involved."

"But you can't be involved." He slammed one hand down on the steering wheel, making her jump. "Did you ever think that the reason you were attacked two nights ago is because whoever did this saw you with me? The closer you get to this case, the more you put yourself in danger. I can't take that risk."

She couldn't believe the words she was hearing. Her heart pounded painfully and she struggled to keep her voice even. "What are you suggesting I do?" she asked.

"Go back to Denver," he said. "I'll make sure you're assigned a victim's advocate, who will keep you informed of anything you need to know about the case."

"So I won't see you again?" She had to force the words past her lips.

"That would be safest," he said.

"Ryan, what's going on?" she asked. "You can't make love to me this morning and then push me away this afternoon."

"We got the forensics report back on your car," he said. "Ethan gave it to me just now."

"The printout he handed you," she said, remembering. "What did they find?"

He blew out a breath. "There was a note in it, on the floorboard. We didn't see it because it was buried under a bunch of windshield glass. It was probably written by whoever vandalized your car."

"What did it say?"

He was silent so long she was ready to demand that he pull over so she could reach out and shake the words out of him. Finally, he said, "The note said, 'I saw you with that cop. I won't let him have you because you're mine.'"

She swallowed hard. "That's not a very specific threat."

"It's still a threat. I won't put you in danger."

"I think I'm safer with you than I am alone."

"You'll be safe in Denver. We can ask the police there to keep an eye on you. You'll be away from the killer."

"I'll be even farther away from my sister." *And away from you.* She wouldn't say the words out loud, afraid they made her too needy. She sat up straighter. "I won't go back to Denver," she said. "Not yet. If you want me to leave your house, I'll find another motel."

He said nothing, and her spirits sank. But she wouldn't give him the satisfaction of letting him see how hurt she was. She would wait until she was alone. Then she'd cry and swear and rant about a man who could steal her heart and so casually hand it back to her.

As SOON AS Ryan pulled into the driveway of his duplex, Jana got out of the car and headed up the walk toward the front door. He caught up with her, grabbing her hand. "Where are you going?" he demanded.

"I'm going to pack."

"No."

"Why not? You said you wanted me away from here—that you didn't want to be responsible. Fine, then. I'll find someplace else to stay."

"No." He pulled her against him and kissed her, a crushing kiss that both seared and soothed. When at last they broke for air, he pushed the hair back from her face. "I was an idiot to think I could let you go."

"You were trying to be noble," she said.

"You didn't think that when I was making my pitch for you to leave. You thought I was a jerk."

"A noble jerk."

He kissed her again. "Stay," he murmured against her lips. "I'll do my best to protect you."

"I know." She pulled back far enough to

smile at him. "And remember, I've got your back, too."

"I feel better already."

"Watch it with the sarcasm, buddy."

"No, I mean it. And you know what would make me feel even better?" He pulled her closer against him.

"Mmm." She nuzzled his neck. "I'll bet I don't need three guesses."

"I love a woman with brains and beauty."

"Come on inside before we embarrass the neighbors." She turned and, giggling, raced inside. Her emotions felt as fragile and unsteady as a soufflé fresh from the oven, but she was determined to stick out this roller-coaster ride. She wasn't going to give up the best thing she had ever had because she had found it in the midst of the worst experience ever.

Chapter Fourteen

"I want to talk to Eric Patterson," Jana announced the next morning over a breakfast of cold cereal and coffee. "I think I'll call him today and try to set up a lunch date."

"What do you want to talk to him about?" Ryan asked. His first instinct was to tell her not to go anywhere near the reporter, but was that his cop sense nudging him—or plain old-fashioned jealousy? After all, Eric had told Jana he didn't want to lose her.

"I'm going to ask him if he's learned anything about Daniel Metwater that might help your case," she said. "After all, he's been spending a lot of time out there at the Prophet's camp."

"I'd planned on setting up an interview with him soon to ask him the same thing," Ryan said. "So you don't need to bother."

Jana set down her coffee cup with a loud

thunk. "I have to do something," she said. "Besides, Eric owes me a date, and he'll probably tell me more than he would the cops."

"What makes you think that?" Ryan asked.

"No offense, but being interviewed by the police is nerve-racking. And remember I told you I thought he wants to be a hero? So he might withhold information that could lead to the Rangers solving the case before he does. But he might not be able to resist the urge to brag about his knowledge to me."

Ryan couldn't argue with her reasoning. "Be careful," he said. "Don't go anywhere alone with the guy."

She looked troubled. "Are you saying he's a suspect in the case?"

"I don't trust him, that's all."

"Neither do I. I figure I'll ask him to meet me someplace downtown—someplace public and crowded. I want information, not an intimate discussion. Though I'd like to know if he put those photos on Jenny's computer, and why."

"Be careful," Ryan said. "If he gets angry, he won't want to help you."

"Provided he knows anything—and that there's anything to know."

"All right. I have to go into work." He pushed

his chair back. "I still don't like leaving you alone, but I get that I can't keep you prisoner."

"My new rental car is being delivered this morning," she said. "And I'll be fine. I promise to be careful."

After a passionate kiss goodbye that could have easily led to more, she locked the door behind him and called Eric Patterson. "Jana!" He sounded pleased to hear from her. "How are you this morning?"

"I'm good, Eric. How are you?"

"Great. The Rangers found Lucia Raton's body yesterday."

"I knew they found a body. Have they definitely identified it as Lucia's?" She was certain Ryan hadn't known this when he left this morning.

"I just got a look at the medical examiner's report. I'm writing up the story right now."

"Do you think you'll have time to break for lunch?" Jana asked. "Considering we couldn't get together the other night."

"That sounds like a great idea. I know your car is out of commission, so let me pick you up. Where are you staying?"

"I'm getting a rental car this morning. Why don't I meet you at Thai Fusion about twelve thirty?"

"Good. And I won't stand you up this time."

She hung up the phone, feeling better about the man. Maybe he was just the type to over-react in certain situations. After all, he was grieving for her sister, too, and she knew well enough that grief could play havoc with a person's emotions.

"You look like something the cat dragged in." Randall greeted Ryan when he arrived at Ranger headquarters. "Rough night?"

"Nothing coffee won't help," he said as he filled his cup.

Between making love with Jana and re-hashing the events of the previous day, Ryan hadn't slept much. The lovemaking had been wonderful—the rehashing painful. He had handled things badly with her, and he wasn't certain she had completely forgiven him yet. The note in her car had sent him into a tail-spin, and he hadn't been thinking clearly.

They had compromised this morning. Jana would stay at his duplex, awaiting the arrival of her new rental car. If she went anywhere, she would let him know of her plans, and she would be sure to stick to public places with other people around. It wasn't an ideal situation, but it was the best he could hope for.

He gathered with the rest of the team in

the conference room. "What's first on the agenda?" Simon asked.

"Let's take another look at the note found in Jana's car." Graham indicated the wrinkled note pinned to the bulletin board. "Is it related to the case or not?"

"I'm assuming 'that cop' is you," Simon said, looking at Ryan.

Ryan ignored the dig. "Whoever wrote that note is watching Jana—or was watching her. Is it our killer?"

"Or maybe a jealous boyfriend?" Randall suggested.

Ryan shook his head. "No boyfriend."

"No prints, no DNA, nothing distinctive about the paper," Graham said. "We'll add it to the file, but don't focus on it for now." He turned to the whiteboard. "We have a positive ID on the body they found yesterday. It is Lucia Raton. She was strangled, though in this case there was no sign of the ligature with the body. The ME suspects some kind of cord or thin rope. Maybe clothesline."

"Same pattern of disposal as Alicia's body," Ethan said. "A shallow grave easily accessed from the road, not much digging involved. Not many people go up there, so not much chance of discovery."

"So odds are the two are related," Ryan said. "What's their connection to the killer?"

"Maybe no relation," Ethan said. "They could be random victims."

"He chose them for some reason," Graham said. "They don't look alike. They aren't the same age, or even the same ethnic background. So what attracted him?"

"They were alone and helpless," Simon said. "That's enough for some predators."

Ryan had left Jana alone. But she wasn't helpless. She wasn't out in the wilderness, far from other people and safety, the way Alicia and Lucia had been. The way Jenny had been.

"How are the background checks on the archaeologists going?" Graham asked.

"So far everyone is clean," Simon said. "No criminal records. A few speeding tickets. Eddleston had a DUI five years back, but he's been clean since. The story about getting back with his wife checks out, too. They're in counseling. Do we focus on Metwater's group next?"

Graham shook his head. "Metwater's lawyers have blocked our access to him and are screaming harassment. The DA wants us to back off until the furor dies down."

"We're federal. We can overrule the DA," Simon said.

"I got a phone call this morning from my boss at the Bureau and he's ordered no fishing expeditions. The only way we can approach Metwater or one of his people is if we have something concrete that links them to the case and warrants our checking them out."

"Are you saying Metwater got to the FBI?" Simon asked.

"He obviously has friends in high places," Graham said. "Let's not forget—before he was a traveling prophet, he was from a rich, powerful family."

"We have to be free to investigate the case," Simon said. "And someone needs to check on Andi Mattheson."

"Why is that?" Ethan asked.

"I think she's at risk for gestational diabetes. She rubs her hands a lot and tingling or numbness in the hands and feet could be a symptom, though the only way to know for sure is with a blood test."

"And you know this how?" Marco asked.

"I volunteered at my uncle's medical clinic when I was a teenager," he said.

"You never cease to amaze me," Marco said.

"Bite me."

"What about the idea to follow up with Eric

Patterson to see if he's uncovered anything?" Graham asked.

"I'm working on that," Ryan said. Or rather, Jana was working on it. Maybe Ryan could find out where they planned to have lunch and just happen to drop by.

"That's all we've got this morning," Graham said. "Let's see if we can't do better today."

Ryan moved out of the conference room to his desk. Once there, he booted up his computer and pulled up the file on Jeremy Eddleston. What had a pretty young girl like Jenny seen in a man who was as plain as dry toast? He appeared to have no interests outside of archaeology. He even spent his weekends giving seminars to area high school students.

Ryan froze and zeroed in on the schedule the university had provided. On July 15, Jeremy Eddleston had given one of his Introduction to Archaeology talks to students at Montrose High School.

The school Lucia Raton had attended.

One week before she died.

Jana accepted the keys to the rental car provided by her auto insurance from the delivery driver and signed the paperwork. The green compact sedan wasn't as flashy as Emma's convertible or as fun as her own vandalized Jeep, but it would get her around town until her car had been repaired, a process her insurance company estimated would take ten days to two weeks now that the impound lot had released the vehicle.

In the meantime, she hoped her lunch with Eric would yield some useful information. She got to the restaurant early and was surprised to find him already waiting by the front door. "So good to see you," he said, hugging her close and kissing her cheek.

She fought the urge to push him away. "Hello, Eric," she said, taking a step back. "Good to see you, too. Why don't we go inside?"

The hostess seated them at a table in the back and presented them with menus. Jana pretended to study hers. "How's work going?" she asked him.

"I am on fire right now," he said. "My editor is loving the stories I'm giving him. Next week I'm going to hit him up for a raise. If I don't get it, I'll walk. With the credits I have lately, I shouldn't have any problem getting a position with a bigger paper. I could be the new Western Slope correspondent for the *Denver Post.*"

"I thought Emma Ellison had that job," Jana said.

"She does now, but if someone better came along, she could be out the door." He grinned. "That's how things work in journalism."

The waitress took their orders and Eric settled back in his chair. "How have you been?" he asked. "How's your head?"

"It's better. Thanks for asking. I saw your profile of Daniel Metwater in the Montrose paper. You did a great job."

"I did, didn't I?" He laughed. "The guy is such a narcissist. All I had to do was ask one question and he was off and running, telling me more than I ever wanted to know about his so-called Family and mission and everything."

She leaned over the table and lowered her voice. "Did you pick up any clues that might point to his involvement with the murders or Jenny's disappearance?" she asked.

"I've got some really incriminating stuff." He sat back as the waitress set their meals in front of them. "I'm not ready to share it yet, but when I do, it will blow the case wide open."

"What did you find out?" she asked, trying—and failing—to rein in her eagerness.

"I can't tell you. Not that I don't want to, but it would be too dangerous."

"Dangerous?"

His eyes met hers, bright and intense. "Metwater has money and connections." He lowered his voice to a whisper. "Some people even say he has ties to the mob. In fact, organized crime may be involved in this case."

"What could organized crime have to do with those two women who died—or with Jenny going missing?" she asked.

"I think they probably saw something at Metwater's camp that they shouldn't have." Eric dug into his Thai basil shrimp. "Metwater didn't have any choice but to eliminate them. Of course, he may not have done the killing himself in every case, but I'm sure he was directing all the action."

Jana felt queasy. "Are you saying he ordered a hit on my sister?"

"I don't have all the proof I need yet, but it's shaping up that way," Eric said. "Of course, we won't know for sure until we find her, so it's important we keep looking. But something tells me these mob guys know how to hide a body where it will never be found."

The mob? It seemed so…surreal.

"Is something wrong with your food?" he asked. "You aren't eating."

She pushed the plate away. "I guess I'm too upset about Jenny."

He nodded and continued forking up shrimp and vegetables. "It is upsetting," he said around a mouthful of shrimp.

How could her sweet, funny, smart sister have ended up with a guy like this? Jana could barely contain her loathing. "Jenny's roommate tells me you stopped by her apartment the other day," she said.

"What, have you been checking up on me?" His smile was lopsided and not convincing.

"I mentioned to her that I had seen a bunch of photos of you and Jenny on Jenny's laptop—I'm sure they weren't there the other day. I thought maybe you had added them."

He shook his head, gaze focused on his meal. "Jenny has always had a lot of pictures of us," he said. "Her screen saver is a shot of us together, if I remember right."

"Eric, those photos weren't there the other day. The Rangers confirmed they weren't there."

"You mean *Ranger*, don't you? I noticed you and Ryan Spencer are getting pretty tight."

"Don't change the subject," she snapped. "What is going on here, Eric?"

"What do you mean, what's going on?"

"Everyone I talked to seemed as surprised as I was to hear of your engagement to Jenny.

Professor Eddleston said he didn't know about it until after Jenny disappeared."

"I told you, we wanted to keep it a secret until Jenny had a chance to tell you." He tapped his fork on the table between them. "We were doing it for you. You should be grateful, not suspicious."

"Jenny's friend Heidi and her roommate, April, say they never heard Jenny say anything about being engaged to you," Jana said. "In fact, April said she didn't think Jenny was that into you."

"They're all liars!"

His shout echoed in the sudden silence. Jana leaned back in alarm. "You need to calm down," she said.

He grabbed his glass of water and downed half of it, his gaze fixed on her, the rage in those eyes frightening her. He set the glass down and wiped his mouth with the back of his hand. "I loved Jenny," he said, his voice even. "It hurts to hear anyone suggest otherwise."

"I didn't say you didn't love her." Jana tried to keep her voice low and non-confrontational. "But maybe the engagement announcement was a little premature? Maybe you intended to ask Jenny to marry you and you never got the chance."

"We were engaged," he said. "I'm sorry if that upsets you, but it's true."

"I'm just trying to figure everything out," she said. "I didn't mean to insult you."

"Jenny means the world to me," he said. "If she's gone, I'll probably never get over her."

Why couldn't she get past the feeling that he said the words like lines in a play? He was playing the part of the grieving lover, but it just didn't ring true.

They finished the meal in silence and Eric claimed the check. "I'll put it on my expense account," he said as he counted out bills. "They can't object to me interviewing the sister of the missing woman, can they?"

He took her arm as they headed toward the parking lot. It took everything in her not to wrench away from him and run to her car. She sagged with relief when she recognized a familiar black-and-white cruiser parked next to her rental. Eric dropped her arm. "What is he doing here?"

Chapter Fifteen

Ryan got out of the cruiser as Jana and Eric approached. Seeing him standing tall and lean in his brown uniform, mirrored sunglasses hiding his eyes, sent a thrill through her. She hurried toward him. "What a nice surprise," she said. Then more softly, "How did you know I was here?"

"The car rental receipt was on the counter at my house, so I kept my eye out for it." He turned to Eric. "How are you, Patterson?"

"Shouldn't you be off investigating something?" Eric asked. "Working the case?"

"I'm always working the case." He kept his focus on Eric until the reporter looked away. Jana had to admit that the sunglasses only added to Ryan's ability to intimidate.

"I have to go," Eric said. "I'll talk to you later, Jana. I'll let you know if I find out anything pertinent."

Ryan watched the reporter until his car turned out of the parking lot. "How did lunch go?" he asked Jana.

"It went pretty much like all my interactions with him," she said. "Odd."

He removed the sunglasses and his eyes met hers, the steady blue gaze instantly settling some of the butterflies in her stomach. "Odd in what way?"

"He thinks Daniel Metwater ordered mob hits on the missing women because they saw something at his camp that they shouldn't have. I'd think he was crazy, except that Emma told me Metwater's brother was supposedly murdered by the mob."

"Supposedly. But nothing points to Metwater's own involvement in organized crime."

"I can't tell if Eric seriously believes the story or if he was making it up for my benefit," she said.

"Did he offer any proof?"

"No. He said he was still gathering his evidence."

"Which means he probably has nothing."

"That's what I thought." She folded her arms under her chest and studied the gravel parking lot. "I asked him about the photos on Jenny's computer, too. He said he didn't put them there, that they've always been there."

"We know that's not true," Ryan said.

She worried her lower lip between her teeth.

"What aren't you telling me?" he asked.

"I may have gone a little too far," she said.

"In what way?"

"I told him I didn't believe he was really engaged to Jenny. I explained how no one seemed to know about the engagement until after she disappeared, and that people who knew Jenny best were surprised by the news. He got really angry."

"You called him a liar. Most people don't respond well to that."

"But what if he is lying?" she asked. "Wouldn't that be important?"

"It would," Ryan agreed. "Which is why we're keeping an eye on him. And we'll dig deeper—try to find out where he was and what he was doing when the other women disappeared."

"When will you know the answers to those questions?" she asked.

"It probably won't be today. We're stretched pretty tight," he said. "I was on my way out to interview Jeremy Eddleston again when I got a call to come into town and talk to a suspect in that plant-theft case Lance has been investigating. I decided that, as long as I was here, I'd see how things were going with you."

"I'm glad you did, seeing you got rid of Eric faster than I probably would have been able to on my own."

"What are your plans for the rest of the afternoon?" he asked as he walked with her to her car.

"I think I'll go back to your place and work," she said. "Maybe dealing with tax accounts will take my mind off Jenny for a little while at least."

"Better you than me." He bent and kissed her gently on the lips. "See you later?"

"I'll be looking forward to it."

That she could have anything to look forward to at a time like this amazed her, but she would take her blessings wherever she could find them and not complain. She had no doubt she could have dealt with Eric Patterson on her own, but she was glad she hadn't had to.

THE NEXT MORNING, Ryan and Ethan headed back to the dig site to question Jeremy Eddleston about his connection to Lucia Raton. "It's a pretty tenuous link," Ethan said as the cruiser bumped along the rutted road to the foot of Mystic Mesa. They had decided to leave Ryan's cruiser at the turnoff so that they could plan their strategy on the way in. "We're still trying to get hold of the registration records for the seminar. Maybe Lucia wasn't even there."

"I still think there's something the professor isn't telling us," Ryan said. "Something about his manner—it's evasive."

"Cops make some people nervous. You know that."

"And some people have reason to be nervous."

When they reached the parking area, the moving truck was gone, and only two cars remained in the lot. The two Rangers left their vehicle and made the trek to the foot of the mesa. "Where is Professor Eddleston?" Ryan asked the two students they found there.

"He…he left about half an hour ago," a young man with a long blond ponytail said.

"You must have passed him on the way out," said his companion, a short young woman with cropped pink hair.

"We didn't pass anyone," Ryan said. He looked to Ethan.

"Hard to miss anyone on these dirt roads," Ethan said. "Though he could have seen us coming and turned onto a side road to wait for us to pass."

"Where was he headed?" Ryan asked.

"Back to the university, I guess," the girl said, wide-eyed.

"Or maybe home," the young man said. "He didn't say. And we didn't ask. He just told us to clean up here and we could leave."

"What's this about?" the girl asked. "Is the professor in some kind of trouble?"

Eddleston was going to be in a lot of trouble when Ryan got hold of him. If it turned out he was the murderer—the man who had attacked Jana—Ryan would do everything in his power to see that he went to prison and never came out. Abruptly, he turned and headed back to the cruiser.

"What do you think?" Ethan asked.

"We could radio the others to search for him," Ryan said.

"But all we know is that he didn't tell us about teaching at Lucia's school," Ethan said. "We don't know if she was in the seminar. Even if she was, he may not have noticed her."

"Why didn't we see him on our way in here?" Ryan stared across the prairie, wondering if Eddleston was sitting in his car out there somewhere, waiting for them to leave.

"Even if he's avoiding us, that just makes him a person of interest," Ethan said. "It doesn't make him guilty."

"But what if he is guilty?" Ryan asked. "What if Lucia was in that seminar and Eddleston noticed her—and that's why she ended up dead?"

JANA WANTED TO get out of the duplex for a while. Being there with Ryan was one thing—he did a good job of distracting her from her circumstances. But being in this unfamiliar place alone made her restless. She still stung from how quickly he had been ready to send her back to Denver two days before. He said he wanted to protect her, but she wasn't some fragile flower or caged bird he could keep under lock and key.

At least he hadn't insisted she stay home today. He had wanted to—she could tell by the way his mouth had tightened when she had told him of her plans for the day, which included getting her hair done and buying a few groceries. Not that she didn't like frozen waffles and cereal, but she wouldn't say no to yogurt for breakfast, and he didn't have a single piece of fruit in the house.

But his mouth tightening had been his only sign of disapproval. Maybe he would relax after she managed to return home tonight unharmed.

She had found a salon that could work her in that morning, so she settled in for some much-needed pampering—a shampoo and trim, and a manicure. She tried not to think of the last time she had visited her sister in Montrose, when she and Jenny had gone together for mani-pedis, talking nonstop about anything and everything as they sat side by side in massage chairs. Every day was full of that kind of memory—eventually, she hoped she would experience them with fondness instead of this aching grief.

After the salon, she headed for the grocery store. While browsing the aisles, she spotted a special on pork loin and decided to make dinner for Ryan. Half an hour later, she headed to her car with four bags of groceries. But rather than go back to the duplex to unload them right away, she turned onto the highway leading out of town. She would take a quick drive to clear her head, then head back and maybe get some work done before she started dinner.

She passed the turnoff to the national park and wondered if Ryan was at Ranger headquarters, or out in the field conducting interviews or tracking down a lead. Her hands tightened on the steering wheel. She hated feeling so powerless to do anything to help. She was the person who knew Jenny the best and loved her the most, yet she had to stand by and let others search for her.

She passed the sign for the Curecanti National Recreation Area and slowed at the turnoff for Mystic Mesa. She could talk to Professor Eddleston again, but she didn't think he was likely to tell her anything he hadn't already told the Rangers.

She could visit Daniel Metwater's camp, maybe pretend to be interested in his teachings. She quickly dismissed the idea as foolish. She was no amateur detective, and snooping where she didn't belong would only get her into trouble.

Instead, she continued on to the lake. Sunlight shimmered on the expanse of blue water, orange cliffs reflected in its mirror-smooth surface. After a few miles she pulled over in a picnic area on the shore. The cluster of tables under metal awnings was deserted, so she sat on one of them and stared out at the water, breathing in the scents of fish and the sagebrush that grew along the rocky shore.

She remembered a boating expedition with her father when she was about twelve and Jenny was six. He liked to fish and would take them out with him, even though they squealed at the idea of baiting hooks with worms and made so much noise they scared all the fish away. He never seemed to mind and said he enjoyed spending time with his girls.

She wished he were with her now. Then again, maybe it was better he hadn't lived to endure the pain of his younger daughter gone missing.

Maybe dead. She drew in a deep, shuddering breath. Was it a betrayal of Jenny to admit that she was very likely gone now? The pain of the idea pierced her, but she forced herself not to shy away from it. For all Ryan's words after they had found Lucia's body had angered her, he had been right that at some point she would need to move on with her life.

Could that be any worse than being caught in this limbo, unable to hope or to mourn?

Another car pulled into the rest area, a tan Camry. She turned and was surprised to see a familiar figure emerge from the vehicle. "What are you doing here?" she asked, annoyed at having her peace disturbed.

"I was looking for you."

"Why?" Maybe the question was rude, but she had no interest in being polite to this man. If she ever did see her sister again, she would ask her why she had ever gotten involved with him.

"We need to talk." He moved around the picnic table toward her. He wore khaki trousers, hiking boots and a blue windbreaker that billowed around him in a gust of wind off the lake. Sunglasses hid his eyes from her.

"We don't have anything to talk about." Something about his manner—the swagger in his walk, perhaps—made her stand and move away. But he was much quicker than she had expected. He lunged forward and grabbed her, yanking her toward him.

"Let go!" she yelped, struggling. "You're hurting me."

"You've hurt me." His fingers dug into her forearms, bruising her. He was much stronger than he looked, and when she kicked at him, he threw her to the ground and knelt on her chest, crushing her.

She stared up at him, terror squeezing her heart and stealing her breath. "What do you want with me?" she gasped.

"I saw you with that cop." He leaned close, his hot breath smelling of onions. "How could you betray me that way?"

"I… I don't know what you're talking about." She heaved against him and tried to roll away, but his crushing weight held her. She arched her neck, searching for help. If only someone would decide to pull in for a break. But not a single car passed on this lonely stretch of highway, and all the boaters were too far away to hear her cries or see what was happening onshore.

"I have to punish you now," he said. He pulled a white cloth from his pocket and wrapped it around her neck. "Goodbye, dearest," he said as he pulled the fabric tight.

Chapter Sixteen

Ryan spent the rest of the morning at Ranger headquarters, trying to track down Jeremy Eddleston. "He's not answering his office or cell phones," he said. "I called the university and no one has seen or heard from him since yesterday morning. His wife insists she hasn't heard from him, either."

"Has she reported him as missing?" Randall asked.

"She said he's probably holed up somewhere in the bowels of the university, cataloging the artifacts from the Mystic Mesa dig," Ryan said. "She doesn't seem terribly concerned."

"I'd think she'd be a little worried if he didn't come home at all, or at least call," Ethan said.

"Apparently, this isn't that unusual," Ryan said. Mrs. Eddleston's exact words had been,

"My husband and I may be married, but we are very independent people. If I called the police every time he decided to spend the night at the university or a dig site instead of coming home they would start labeling me a nuisance."

"You interviewed her already, right?" Ethan asked.

"Yes," Ryan said. "She's got a solid alibi for the afternoon Jenny disappeared—she was at a marriage counselor's office."

"Was she surprised to learn her husband was involved with Jenny?" Ethan asked.

"No. Her husband may have thought she was in the dark, but I got the impression there wasn't much he did that she didn't know about."

"Was he telling the truth about their reconciliation?" Ethan asked.

"I think so." She hadn't struck Ryan as the type who would cover up for her husband. "She didn't come right out and say it, but she certainly implied that most of the money in the marriage is hers. He probably doesn't want to give that up to live on a professor's salary."

"So where is our professor?" Randall asked.

"I think he's avoiding us," Ryan said. He swiveled his chair around and stretched. "But odds are he'll turn up at the university or home eventually, and we'll corner him. In the meantime, let's put him aside and focus on another suspect."

"Who?" Ethan asked.

"I want to dig a little deeper into Eric Patterson's background," Ryan said.

"He says he was working at the paper the afternoon Jenny disappeared," Ethan said. "No one there specifically remembers him being there that day, but no one will say he wasn't, either. Reporters are in and out of the office all day. His work computer does show he was logged in at the time."

"But computer records can be faked," Ryan said.

"He's got a definite link to Jenny Lassiter," Randall said. "But can we prove he knew Lucia or Alicia?"

"Maybe we should take a closer look at the articles he's written for the paper," Ethan said. "Maybe he did a story where he interviewed high school students."

"I don't see how he could have known Alicia," Ryan said. "And her killing feels more like a crime of opportunity—the wrong guy finds her lost in the desert and strangles her. Maybe because she refused his advances, maybe just for the thrill of it."

"Which brings us back to Daniel Metwater

or Jeremy Eddleston," Randall said. "Both of them were in the area where Alicia became separated from her group."

"I hate cases like this," Ethan said. "After a while, everyone looks like a suspect."

"And we could be dealing with more than one suspect," Randall said.

"Where's a script writer when you need one?" Ethan said. "They always manage to tie everything up neatly on TV."

"Good to see you all so hard at work." Simon came in and dumped his backpack on his desk.

"We're brainstorming," Randall said. "You got any new leads for us?"

"Maybe." He took a file from his bag and carried it over to them. "We finally got hold of the roster for the Introduction to Archaeology Saturday seminar at Montrose High School," he said. "Luisa Raton is on it."

"Whoa." Randall grabbed the folder and scanned it. "So she and Eddleston did have contact."

"One of the teachers who was there tells me Lucia sat up front and asked a lot of questions," Simon said. "No way Eddleston could have missed seeing her."

"I think we need to pay another visit to Mrs. Eddleston," Ethan said. "Let's push a little harder and find out what she knows, and if she's heard from her husband."

JANA WOKE TO darkness and pain. Her throat ached so that it was agony to swallow. She was curled in a fetal position, jostled back and forth, some new misery blossoming with each movement. As her eyes adjusted to the dimness, she realized she was in a car trunk, her back pressed against the spare tire. She lay on something scratchy, maybe an old blanket. Just enough light seeped in around the trunk to show the direness of her situation.

Carefully, trying not to make any noise, she uncurled her body as much as possible and reached up to her throat. Something was wrapped around her neck but had loosened. She tugged, freeing a long strip of some lightweight fabric, and gasped, taking her first deep breath in who knew how long. Her throat still ached, but the knowledge of how close she had come to dying, yet had survived, sent a surge of adrenaline through her.

Think, she commanded herself. She needed to assess her situation. She was in the trunk of a car. It was traveling pretty fast and there wasn't a lot of road noise, so they were probably still on pavement—the highway, then. She didn't know how long she had been unconscious, but probably not very long. Her attacker had strangled her with the cloth, then dumped her in the car trunk. He hadn't bound her hands or feet, which told her he had probably assumed she was dead or dying. Now he was taking her where? To dispose of her body?

Horror at the thought sent a shudder through her, but she forced her mind back to the problem at hand. She could freak out later, but not now. Now she had to keep her wits about her. She studied the interior of the car trunk again. Hadn't she read that car trunks had interior releases, in case a child crawled inside and got stuck? She felt along the sides until she found a rough place that might have once been the latch, but it wasn't there. Had it broken accidentally—or had the driver of the car deliberately filed it off?

She felt faint at the thought and once again fought for control. She knew the man who had tried to strangle her was the murderer, and that he had probably killed Jenny. Her sister would have trusted him—would have probably willingly gone with him anywhere.

She blinked back tears and felt all about her for a weapon. Her fingers closed around a folding shovel—the kind people kept in their cars for digging out of snow. A tire iron would have been better, but maybe this was the kind of car with the tire tools tucked in a recess under the trunk floor. The shovel would have to do for now.

Her captor thought she was dead. When he opened the trunk, he wouldn't be expecting her to leap out. She would hit him in the face as hard as she could with the shovel, hopefully breaking his nose.

And then what? She had no idea where he was taking her. Running blindly into the woods wouldn't help her. Even if she ran to the road, she had no guarantee anyone would come by who would help her.

She would have to use this car to drive away. She would have to keep hitting the man until he was unconscious. Then she would take his keys—or maybe she would get lucky and he would have left them in the ignition—and she would try to find a main road and follow it to a gas station or somewhere with a phone. Then she would call Ryan. She wouldn't even mind if he said *I told you so.*

"I DON'T KNOW where my husband is, Officer." Melissa Eddleston was a slim blonde in her early fifties, with bright blue eyes and elegant features. The homely professor must have something going on, Ryan thought, to have landed yet another beauty. He'd been tagged with interviewing Mrs. Eddleston again, while Ethan and Randall headed to the university.

"I told you before, he's probably sitting in the basement somewhere, lost in cataloging his finds from the dig site," she said. "Have you looked for him there?"

"We have two officers there now," Ryan said. "But so far they haven't located him. He's not at the dig site, and he isn't answering his phone. He hasn't logged on to the computer at the university since yesterday morning."

"I'm sorry to say, Jeremy is the epitome of the clichéd absentminded professor," Mrs. Eddleston said. "He often turns off his phone when he is involved in his work. Trust me, he's somewhere delighting in pottery shards and broken sandals."

Ryan looked around the living room of the spacious home on a private golf course. Twin white leather sofas flanked a brass-and-glass cocktail table. Gold-upholstered side chairs and gold-and-white lamps made the room look elegant and somewhat sterile. Not the kind of place where most men would be comfortable, he thought. "Where did the professor live while the two of you were separated?" he asked.

She pressed her lips together. "I don't know what that has to do with anything."

"I'm trying to think where else he might go."

"He had an apartment over on Fifth. It's the kind of cheap place filled with students and the newly divorced. He hated it. I'm sure he wouldn't go back there."

"Was your husband's affair with Jennifer Lassiter the first time he cheated on you?"

Her face paled and her nostrils flared. "I'm not sure you can call it *cheating* when a couple is legally separated," she said, the words crisp and clipped.

"Before you were separated, had he ever cheated on you?" Ryan kept his eyes on her, showing no mercy. He needed the answer to his questions, no matter how uncomfortable they made her.

"I don't see how that question is relevant."

"The fact that you don't want to answer makes me think your husband had strayed before," he said.

She bowed her head, some of the starch drained from her posture. "Once that I know of for sure," she said. "Though I suspected a couple of other times. It's why I wanted the separation. But Jeremy is older and wiser now.

He's working with our counselor. I'm quite sure he is sincere in his desire to be faithful."

"Were his other lovers all young women like Jennifer?" Ryan asked.

"He's a professor. He's surrounded by young women. They throw themselves at him." She sniffed. "She certainly did."

"You're aware that Jennifer Lassiter is missing," Ryan said.

"I am. But I can promise you Jeremy had nothing to do with that."

"How can you be so sure?"

"Because he was with me the afternoon she went missing. He left the dig site early for our first counseling appointment."

"What time was the appointment?" According to Jenny's coworkers, she had gone for a walk about one o'clock.

"The appointment was from two to three in the afternoon. I told you this before."

"You told me you were at a marriage counselor's that afternoon. You didn't mention your husband."

"Didn't I?" She waved her hand dismissively. "It doesn't matter. He was there. We went for coffee afterward, then came home and stayed here the rest of the evening."

To make a two-o'clock appointment, Eddleston would have had to leave the dig site by one fifteen. The last time any of Jenny's coworkers could remember having seen her had been one o'clock. Not a lot of time to kidnap someone, perhaps kill them and hide the evidence.

"And your husband was with you the whole time, from two until the next morning?" Ryan asked.

She frowned, tiny lines radiating from the corners of her eyes.

"Mrs. Eddleston, I can bring you in for questioning if I feel you're withholding information," he said.

"He was late for our appointment," she said. "Not very—maybe twenty minutes. He said he got involved in his work. I believed him. I *believe* him. Why are you asking these questions?"

"Are you aware that another young woman— a high school student—went missing a couple of weeks before Jennifer disappeared? A girl named Lucia Raton?"

"I heard news reports about it, yes."

"Did you know that your husband knew Lucia?"

"What?" There was no mistaking her alarm. "How? A high school student? He wouldn't—"

"He taught a Saturday seminar, an introduction to archaeology, at her high school."

"He teaches many of those seminars. He enjoys introducing young people to archaeology."

"He never mentioned Lucia to you?"

"Why would he? He may have had a weakness for young women, but never a girl that young. Officer, we have two daughters!"

"What about Alicia Mendoza. Did he ever mention her?"

"No. I don't know that name."

"There's no need to badger my wife, Officer."

They both turned to find Jeremy Eddleston standing in the archway leading to the living room. His face was gray and drawn, and he looked at least ten years older than when Ryan had first seen him at the dig site. He took a step into the room. "I know you've been looking for me," he said. "I'm ready to tell you everything."

Chapter Seventeen

The car had turned onto a dirt road, the ride suddenly much slower and rougher. Jana tried to brace herself inside the trunk, but at every bump and curve she was thrown painfully against the sides. She gritted her teeth, trying not to cry out, terrified her captor would hear her and know she was still alive.

She rolled back toward the bumper and was wedged there. The car was climbing an incline. Were they headed back to the old logging site? Maybe the killer reasoned since the Rangers had found Lucia Raton's body, they wouldn't return there to look for another.

She didn't know how many minutes passed before the car stopped, but it seemed a long time. She grabbed the shovel and braced herself. The car door opened, then slammed shut, the sound hollow from inside the trunk. Footsteps moved around the side of the car, crunching in the gravel. She heard the scrape of the key in the lock and braced herself. The narrow band of light widened as the lid began to rise and she lifted the shovel, ready to strike.

"Oh, no, you don't!" The killer grabbed her with both hands and dragged her from the vehicle, forcing the shovel out of her grasp and banging her knees painfully against the edge of the trunk. She struggled against him, terror lending her strength.

He released one hand long enough to strike her, a hard blow to the side of the head that left her reeling and tasting blood where she had bit her lip. She struggled to steady herself and stared at him. Her mind raced with things she wanted to say to him—vile curses to hurl at him or horrible accusations. Instead, she said, "What did you do to Jenny? Where is my sister?"

He smiled, an expression that made her sick to her stomach. "I loved Jenny," he said. "But she wouldn't love me. I told her I would take care of her—that we could be together forever, but she said she couldn't be with someone like me."

"What did you do to her?"

"The same thing I did to Lucia and Alicia. The same thing I'm going to do to you."

He still held her with only one hand. She tried to pull away, but his fingers closed around her wrist even tighter, so that she feared her bones might snap. "Why did you kill them?" she asked.

"I had to make sure I did it right when it came time to take care of Jenny," he said. "So I had to practice. I picked up Lucia when she was hitchhiking. I was on my way to see Metwater and she was just leaving his camp, so I turned around and offered her a ride. I took her for coffee. She was unhappy and wanted to run away from home. I saw that I could help her. She's not unhappy anymore. She's not anything."

Jana's stomach lurched. Her throat and her wrist screamed in pain, but she fought to keep a clear head. The longer she kept him talking, the more time she was buying herself. "What about Alicia?" she asked.

"I wasn't planning on killing her, but I saw her walking along the road and decided it wouldn't hurt to try again—just to make sure I had perfected my technique." He frowned. "I had tried one other time, with Andi Mattheson—Daniel Metwater's pet—but she got away. I didn't want to risk that happening with Jenny."

She stared at him. Clearly he was insane,

which made him all the more frightening. How did you reason with someone like that?

"I failed with Andi," he continued. "But she gave me the idea to frame Metwater. He thinks he's so superior, all those women fawning over him. The Rangers hate him anyway, so it was almost too easy to make them see him as the culprit. I planted that torn shirt in his closet and they went after it like dogs on a meaty bone. They never even thought to look at me. After all, I'm harmless." His laughter sent an icy chill through her. "You know another great thing about all of this?" he continued. "I'm getting some great newspaper stories out of it. I wouldn't be surprised if I didn't win at least one Associated Press award for my series on the serial killer who's terrorizing this sleepy little county. This could be the break I need to move on to a really great job with one of the major media outlets. I guess it's true what they say—the people who get ahead are the ones who help themselves."

His words made her physically ill, but she had to keep him talking. She had no idea what time it was, but if she could stall until Ryan returned to the condo, he would be alarmed that she was missing and would come looking for her. She knew the odds of him ever locating her on this deserted side road were slim, but it was the best chance she had of getting out of this alive.

"You attacked me that night at Jenny's apartment," she said.

"I was interrupted." He tightened his hold on her again. "But now I'm going to finish what I started."

"No!" she screamed, startling him. His grip on her weakened just enough for her to pull away. He lunged after her, his fingers grabbing at the hem of her shirt. She heard the fabric tear and stumbled with the forward momentum of the sudden release. Gravel bit into her palms as she shoved herself up again and started running, feet scrabbling for purchase, her pursuer's shouts sending shudders through her.

"You can't get away from me!" he screamed. "There's nowhere for you to run!"

JEREMY EDDLESTON SLUMPED onto one of the white leather sofas while Ryan took a seat on the other. Mrs. Eddleston perched on the far end of her husband's sofa, eyeing both men warily. "Were you aware I've been trying to reach you since yesterday?" Ryan asked.

"Yes." Eddleston's shoulders sagged further. "I saw the cruiser headed toward the dig site yesterday and I turned into a side canyon and waited until you'd passed. I figured you were coming for me—that you'd found out my secret. I've spent the past twenty-four hours driving around, trying to think what to do. I spent the night in my car, parked behind a deserted gas station somewhere in the middle of nowhere." He ran a hand over his unshaven chin. "I didn't sleep much. I knew if you talked to enough people, you'd eventually find out the truth. I decided I had better come clean before I dug my grave any deeper."

His choice of words sent a chill through Ryan. "What do you have to tell me?" he asked.

"I lied when I said I hadn't seen Jenny the afternoon she disappeared. I did see her."

Ryan waited. Silence often coaxed more from people than additional questions.

Eddleston looked sideways at his wife, who refused to meet his gaze. "I left work early that afternoon," he said. "Around twelve. I met a friend for lunch at the café out by the lake."

"A friend?" Mrs. Eddleston coated the words in ice.

"We were lingering over coffee when Jenny came in with Eric Patterson," Eddleston said. "She didn't look happy, and almost as soon as they sat down they began arguing."

Ryan tamped down the anger that surged

in him. "Why didn't you tell us this before?" he asked.

Eddleston glanced at his wife again. "Because I knew if I did, word would get back to Melissa."

"Who was the woman this time?" Melissa Eddleston asked. "Another one of your students?"

"It doesn't matter," he said. "It's over between us. I promise."

"Your promises mean nothing to me anymore. Who was she?"

He pressed his lips together, bleaching them of all their color.

Ryan pulled out a notepad. "I'll need the name in order to corroborate your story," he said.

He sent his wife another pained look. "Lisa Cole. She's an adjunct history professor at the college."

Melissa gave a muffled cry, stood and fled from the room. Eddleston stared after her. "I don't think she'll forgive me this time," he said.

"What happened with Jenny and Eric?" Ryan asked.

Eddleston dragged his attention back to Ryan. "They argued for ten minutes or so. She said something about how she wanted him to leave her alone. He kept saying he loved her and they belonged together. Finally, she shouted that she didn't love him and stormed out. He rushed after her."

"Did they leave together?" Ryan asked.

"I don't know. When Lisa and I paid our check and left about five minutes later, they were gone."

"What about Lucia Raton?" Ryan asked.

Eddleston blinked. "What about her?"

"She attended the Introduction to Archaeology seminar you presented at Montrose High School a few days before she disappeared."

"Did she? I'm sorry, I don't remember."

"She was a very pretty girl. She sat near the front and asked a lot of questions."

"Maybe…" He shook his head. "I do so many of those presentations. They all run together after a while."

"So you don't remember a pretty young girl who was fascinated by you and your subject matter?"

Eddleston shook his head. "I have my weaknesses, but children are not one of them."

"I'm going to ask you again—did you have any kind of encounter with Lucia Raton—did you see her or talk to her or have any idea what happened to her?"

"No. I promise I never laid eyes on her." He

looked up at Ryan through his bushy brows. "I didn't hurt Jenny," he said. "She was my friend. I know you don't believe me, but it's true. And I tried to be a friend to her. She seemed to need that."

"Why did she need a friend?" Ryan asked. "Didn't she have friends her own age?"

"I don't know," Eddleston said. "But she said she liked being with me because she always felt safe." He sighed. "I don't like to believe this because it hurts my ego, but Jenny told me her father died when she was still quite young. Maybe she saw me as a kind of father figure."

Ryan put away his notebook and stood. "What happens now?" Eddleston asked.

"You probably want to find a good divorce lawyer," Ryan said.

"You're not going to charge me?" the professor asked. "I withheld evidence."

"You did, but I'm not going to charge you. And while infidelity is distasteful, it isn't against the law."

Back in the cruiser, Ryan telephoned Ethan. His fellow Ranger must have been out of cellphone range; Ryan had to leave a message on his voice mail summarizing his interview with Eddleston. "I'm going to follow up with the girlfriend," he said. "But I have a feeling the professor is telling us the truth this time."

He ended the call and prepared to telephone the commander when his phone buzzed. He checked the screen and answered. "Simon, what's up?" he asked.

"Where are you?" Simon asked. "Where's Jana?"

"Jana's at my condo." She had mentioned doing some shopping that morning, but surely she was back by now. "Why?"

"You need to get hold of her. I think she's in danger."

Ryan started the cruiser and put it into gear, thoughts racing. "Why is she in danger?" he demanded. "What have you found out?"

"I went out to Daniel Metwater's camp this morning," Simon said. "I talked to Andi Mattheson. She told me who Easy is."

"Easy?" Ryan turned the cruiser onto the highway, headed toward his duplex.

"The man who was seen with Lucia Raton before she died. Metwater had ordered his followers not to talk about him, but I persuaded Andi to tell me. Easy is Eric Patterson."

"What?"

"Easy is Eric Patterson. He isn't some reporter who just decided to do a profile of Daniel Metwater. He's been hanging around the camp for weeks now."

"Why do you think Jana is in danger?"

"Andi says Eric was never engaged to Jenny Lassiter. He bought her a ring but she wouldn't accept it. Andi saw them arguing about it one day a couple of weeks before Jenny disappeared. She said lately he's been talking about Jana the same way he used to talk about Jenny—about how they were meant to be together forever."

Ryan flipped the switch to activate his lights and siren and pressed down hard on the accelerator. "I'm going to find Jana," he said. "I hope to God we aren't too late."

JANA FELL, SLIDING down the steep slope, rocks tearing her jeans and ripping long gashes in her arms. "Give up now!" Eric shouted above her. "You'll never get away from me."

Shards of rock exploded to her left and she looked back to see him standing at the top of the incline, a pistol in his hand. He raised it and aimed toward her.

Panicked, she levered herself up and ran to the side, into a tangle of twisted pines and juniper. She tripped on roots and rolled her ankles on rocks, but terror drove her forward. She had no idea where she was or how far behind her Eric was, but she had to keep moving. She wouldn't let him kill her. She wouldn't die.

After several minutes, though, she had to stop. Her lungs burned and every breath was a struggle. She pressed her back against the trunk of an ancient pine and studied the shadowed woodland for any sign of her pursuer. She saw nothing and heard nothing but her own ragged breathing. Not so much as a bird chirped in the stillness.

She felt for her phone in her pocket. Amazingly, it hadn't been crushed in her mad scramble. Unfortunately, the screen showed not a single bar of service. She pressed the 9-1-1 buttons anyway, hoping against hope that somehow the signal would make it through the ether. She had heard law-enforcement could track people by their cell phones. But in order to track someone, they would have to know a person was missing. As far as anyone knew, she was still happily shopping in Montrose. Who knew when Ryan would arrive home and find her missing? He might have to work late on the case, and by the time he missed her, it would be too late.

Would someone see her car at the picnic area and report an abandoned vehicle? How long would it take for that report to make its way to Ryan? She swallowed a lump in her throat. If he knew she was in danger, she was certain he would come to her rescue. If only he knew.

Chapter Eighteen

Ryan called up Jana's number on his phone and waited impatiently while it rang and rang. "You have reached the voice mailbox of…"

"Jana, it's Ryan. Answer me now. It's important."

No one picked up and he angrily ended the call and tossed the phone onto the console. Where was she? He pressed his foot to the floor, the siren wailing. He scarcely slowed for the turnoff to his condo, tires squealing as he braked for the approach to his driveway. But he saw long before he arrived that the drive was empty. The green rental car she had gotten yesterday wasn't in the garage or parked on the street.

He made himself stop the cruiser, get out and go inside. "Jana!" he shouted, hearing the panic in his voice. "Jana, are you here?"

No answer. He raced back to his vehicle

and called her cell again. When the voice-mail message came on, he ended the call and punched in the number of Ranger headquarters. "What's going on there?" he asked when Randall Knightbridge picked up the phone.

"Simon and I went by the newspaper office, hoping to surprise Eric Patterson," Randall said. "His editor said he hadn't been in that morning, even though there was a mandatory editorial meeting. We checked his apartment and he wasn't there, either."

Ryan swore. Of course, that would have been too easy.

"We've got an APB out on him," Randall said. "Simon and Marco headed back to Metwater's camp in case Patterson shows up there, and we've got people at the newspaper, and at his apartment."

"I'll head to the Lakeside Café," Ryan said. "Eddleston says Eric was with Jenny there the afternoon she disappeared. I'll see if I can get a positive ID on him as the man who was there with Lucia before she died. Has anyone heard from Jana?"

"Sorry, no. You haven't seen her?"

"No."

"We'll keep looking," Randall said. "Hang in there."

He didn't ask why Randall would say that.

His feelings for Jana must have been obvious to his coworkers even if he hadn't found the courage to share them with Jana. If he saw her again—*when* he saw her again—he would tell her how much he loved her and how he never wanted her to leave him.

No cars sat in the café lot, though he spotted two vehicles around back, neither of them Eric Patterson's Camry. He parked and went inside. Mary looked up from a magazine as he entered. "Hello, Officer," she said. "Back for more of my coffee?"

"I'm looking for someone." He pulled up a photo of Eric Patterson and showed it to her. "Do you recognize this man?"

She tilted her head a little as she studied the photo, then nodded. "He could be the guy," she said.

Ryan's gut clenched. "What guy?"

"The one who was with that missing girl."

"And you're sure he hasn't been in here since then," Ryan asked.

She shrank back a little and he realized he had barked the question. He took a deep breath, telling himself to stay calm. "Someone else said they saw him in here a few days ago with a different young woman," he said.

"Oh, well, that would have been when I went

to visit my sister over in Westminster," Mary said. "I was away for five days last week."

"Who worked while you were away?" Ryan asked.

"Bernadette came in two days and Shelly worked the other three," Mary said.

"I'll need their contact information," Ryan said. "I may want to talk to them." He glanced around the empty café. "You're sure the man in that photo hasn't been by here today."

"No, honey. Just the usual fishermen and a couple of campers and some highway workers." She began writing on the back of an order pad. "Here's how to get in touch with Bernadette and Shelly."

"What about this woman?" Ryan showed her a photo of Jana. "Have you seen her?"

Mary shook her head. "Not since she was here with you yesterday. She's pretty, isn't she? Is she a special friend of yours?"

"Yes." Jana was a special friend. He hoped he got the opportunity to tell her so.

He took the piece of paper Mary handed him with the waitresses' contact information and handed her one of his cards. "Call me right away if the man or the woman I showed you come in here," he said.

"Sure thing." She placed the card on the counter beside the register. "Hang on one second."

She left and returned shortly with a to-go cup. "You look like you could use some coffee for the road," she said. "No charge. And I hope you find your friend."

Ryan headed down the road, unsure what he was looking for. All he knew was that Eric Patterson had probably buried two other women in this area. Jenny Lassiter was most likely dead, also. Ryan didn't know if Eric had killed the women where he had found them, or brought them out here to do the deed—he hoped the latter. He needed to believe that Jana was still alive, that he still had time to save her.

He passed the turnoff that led up to the old logging site. A forensics team had searched the area and found no more graves. Eric had left Alicia Mendoza in a drainage ditch dug by highway contractors. Where else in the area would Ryan find disturbed ground that the killer might consider suitable for disposing of a body?

A flash of dark green caught his eye as he passed a picnic area and he braked hard and swung the cruiser into a sharp U-turn. He was calling in the plate on the vehicle before he had even come to a stop, but he already knew what the answer to his query would be. Phone to his ear, he climbed out and approached the car.

"That vehicle is registered to VIP Rentals," the woman on the other end of the phone said.

Ryan didn't need to hear more. He slipped the phone back into his pocket and hastily put on latex gloves. Then he tried the driver's door. The car was unlocked. Before he even had the door opened, he recognized Jana's purse on the front seat.

He checked the rest of the car. Four bags of groceries in the trunk. The meat was still cool to the touch, so it hadn't been sitting there too long. But how long?

Leaving the car, he walked toward the closest picnic table. He hadn't gone far before he saw the drag marks—parallel lines in the dust leading from the concrete pad for the picnic table to the parking lot. They ended abruptly, a couple of feet from faint tire treads. Ryan knelt to study the treads. He guessed they were passenger-car tires, though he was no expert. Whether they came from Eric Patterson's Camry he couldn't say, but he didn't like the odds that they weren't a match for Patterson's car.

He pulled out his phone again and called Ranger headquarters. This time fellow officer Michael Dance answered. "I found Jana's car," Ryan said. "It's at a picnic area by the lake. There are signs of a struggle in the parking lot and some tire treads. We need to get someone out here to take photos and measurements. And we need to start a search for her, right away."

"Carmen's free. I'll send her," Michael said. "And we'll get everyone we can to start searching. Where are you off to now?"

"I don't know. I'll let you know when I get there."

Ryan returned to his car and pulled out a Forest Service map. It showed all the roads, trails, rest areas and campgrounds in this area. He found a pen and circled the logging site where Lucia's body had been found and the stretch of road construction where the workmen had discovered Alicia. He studied the mass of roads, streams and contour lines between the two and zeroed in on a road marked Private, Admittance by Permit Only. He traced the road up a series of closely spaced contour lines until it ended at a pair of crossed pickaxes. The symbol for a mine.

His heart skipped a beat. A mine could mean an old adit or shaft. The perfect place to dispose of a body.

ERIC DIDN'T BOTHER trying to sneak up on Jana. He crashed through the woods with all the subtlety of a moose, crunching leaves and snapping twigs announcing his approach. "You won't get away from me," he said. "When I want something, I don't give up."

She didn't give up, either. She wasn't going to let fear or his bullying and threats make her surrender without a fight. She pushed off from the tree trunk she had been resting against and began running again. She hoped she was moving back toward the road. If she could get to the car before he did, she might have a chance of getting away.

She hadn't gone too far before she realized she could no longer hear Eric crashing through the trees behind her. And he wasn't firing in her direction. Had she been lucky enough to lose him? She slowed her pace to a trot, straining her ears for any sounds of approach. Glancing back over her shoulder, she saw nothing but the bleached trunks of aspen, jutting up from the ground like the quills of a porcupine.

She slowed more, still moving but allowing herself to catch her breath. If only she had a cell phone signal, she could use a mapping app to figure out where she was. Of course, if her phone worked, she could summon help and she wouldn't be in this fix.

She started forward again, but stopped abruptly, loose rock sliding from beneath her shoes, bounding and echoing as it descended into a deep canyon. She stared down at the sheer drop at her feet. Sun glinted on a narrow stream of water far below and sparkled on threads of quartz in the vertical rock slabs.

"Watch that last step, it's a big one."

She turned and saw the gun pointed at her, then the man behind it. Eric was close enough now that he wouldn't miss if he fired. He closed the gap between them and grabbed her arm. "I told you you wouldn't get away from me," he said, and tugged her back the way she had come.

"Where are you taking me?" she asked as she stumbled along beside him.

"I'm taking you to join your sister. You can be with her forever now. That's what you want, isn't it?"

His words, and the almost gleeful way he said them, made her knees weak. She stumbled and almost fell.

Eric yanked her upright and pressed the barrel of the gun into her side. "Don't try anything stupid," he said. "I don't want to have to kill you yet, but I will."

Which meant he would eventually kill her if she didn't escape from him first. He had already proved she couldn't outrun him. He apparently knew the area well. She pictured him exploring the area, planning his crimes. Planning to murder the woman he claimed to love.

Could she wrestle the gun away and turn it on him? She doubted it. His finger was too close to the trigger. One wrong move from her and he'd simply fire it. A bullet at this short range would be devastating.

She could try to trip him, but he held her so tightly he would only bring her down with him. She wished she knew judo or some other martial art, where she might have learned how to use an opponent's own weight against him.

It's hopeless, a voice whispered in her head.

No! she answered back. Everything she had read told her the people who survived against the odds were the ones who didn't give up. She wouldn't give up.

They left the woods and started up the rocky slope she had descended earlier. "Where are we going?" she asked.

"I told you, I'm taking you to join your sister."

"Yes, but where?" she said.

He chuckled. "You're just like her, you know? She was curious, too. Always asking me questions. What are you doing? Why are you doing that? Where are we going? It's one of the things I liked about her, actually. She was so smart and inquisitive. She would have made a good reporter."

Hearing him talk about Jenny this way made her stomach churn with rage. If she could have martialed her anger into a weapon, she would have engulfed him in flames. "So where are you taking me?" she asked again, hoping if she learned the answer it would help her plan an escape.

"Look down at your feet," he said. "Tell me what you see."

She looked down. "I see rocks." Her knees and arms still ached from falling on this jagged scree, some of the rocks the size of her fist, others as big as her head.

"It's mine waste," he said. "From the Molly May mine. They pulled a lot of gold out of here in the 1870s, but no one comes up here anymore."

"You're taking me to a mine?" Her spirits sank. Colorado was riddled with old mines from which men had extracted—some with more success than others—gold, silver, copper, iron, coal and other minerals over the years. When the mines stopped yielding their riches they were abandoned, left to fill with water and debris. The more accessible were covered with iron barriers or grates to keep out unwary passing animals and people, but those higher in the mountains, off the beaten path, remained open.

The perfect place to dispose of a body. She swallowed a surge of nausea.

"Come on." Eric tugged on her arm. "I haven't got all day."

Weathered timbers came into view above them and proved to be a roughly framed hut that formed the entrance to the mine. She dug in her heels, holding back. "I don't want to go in there," she said.

She expected another outburst of anger, but Eric turned to her with surprising tenderness. "It's not far," he said. "Only about fifty yards in before we get to the first shaft. Jenny is waiting for you there. Won't you be happy to see her?"

Jana bit her lip, afraid she was going to cry. She didn't want to give him the satisfaction of knowing he had broken her. "I don't like the dark," she said, which wasn't a lie.

"You don't have to worry," Eric said. "I know the way."

"It's still dark." She hoped she didn't sound as pathetic as she felt.

He released his hold on her arm, but kept the gun pressed into her side, then reached into his pocket and pulled out a Mini Maglite. "See," he said. "I think of everything. Now come on."

RYAN GUNNED THE cruiser up the rough mining road, tires slipping and rocks ringing on the undercarriage. He kept his foot pressed to the accelerator, wrestling the steering wheel to keep the vehicle on the narrow track. More than once the SUV slid dangerously close to the drop-off beside the road, but he somehow kept going. Now wasn't the time for caution; he only prayed he wasn't too late.

He'd called for backup from the picnic area, then headed for the turnoff, lights and siren off in case Eric was close enough to see or hear and be alerted to his approach. He wasn't sure how he was going to deal with Patterson, but he would assess the situation when he found the murderer.

Sun glinted off metal ahead. Ryan slowed as he recognized Eric Patterson's Camry. The trunk was open, a yellow plastic snow shovel on the ground in front of it. Ryan parked behind the Camry, angling the cruiser sideways to block it in. He shut off the engine and studied the scene. A footpath led up the slope away from the car, probably to the mine, though he had no idea how far away that might be.

A soft breeze rustled the trees that had grown up close to the little clearing, bringing in the scent of pine and the music of birdsong. Under other circumstances, this would have been an idyllic scene. But a sense of dread colored the atmosphere with gloom.

Ryan drew his Glock and eased over to the cover of the trees. Moving as swiftly as possible yet trying not to make any noise, he began climbing the slope. After five minutes of climbing, the modest entrance to a mine adit emerged from the side of the mountain, the opening a black mouth framed by silvered timbers.

He crossed the gap between the trees and the mine opening on a run, ducking around the side of the timbers for cover. Waiting for his breathing to slow, he strained his ears to listen.

The low murmur of voices, too garbled to make out words, drifted from the opening. Heart pounding, Ryan ducked inside. He plastered himself against one side of the tunnel, damp seeping through the rocks soaking into his shirt. Carefully placing each step, he inched along the wall, toward a faint light that glowed in the distance.

The voices became clearer as he neared the light. "Stand there, with your back to the shaft," a man—Eric Patterson—said.

"What are you going to do?" Jana's voice trembled with fear. Ryan forced himself not to react. He inched closer, weapon raised.

"I'm trying to make this easy for you," Eric said. "If you cooperate this will be a much better experience."

"You're going to kill me," Jana said. "How can that in any way be a good experience?"

"Look, if you don't cooperate, I'll just push you in and you can starve to death down there. Would you like that better?"

Ryan didn't need to hear any more. "Eric Patterson, freeze!" he shouted, and rushed forward to the end of the corridor. Patterson turned and fired, his bullet striking the rock wall beside Ryan's right shoulder, sending granite shards flying.

Jana screamed and dropped to the ground on one side of the open shaft. Eric turned and aimed his weapon not at Ryan, but at her. "Come any closer and I'll kill her," he said.

"Then you'll die, too," Ryan said. "Is that what you want?"

"You should never have interfered," Eric said. "If you hadn't tried to take Jenny from me I never would have had to resort to this."

"I didn't know Jenny," Ryan said.

"Don't lie to me!" Eric barked, and shifted the gun to aim at Ryan. "First it was that professor—what did she ever see in that ugly old man? I thought I had fixed that. I made it to where she could never leave me again. Then you came along and I saw you kissing her. It made me sick. You should have left well enough alone."

"Put the gun down," Ryan said. "You won't solve anything by killing anyone."

"Don't come any closer!" Eric leveled the pistol at Ryan, who dived for the ground as the shot exploded in the small space, the sound reverberating painfully in his ears, the smell of cordite stinging his nose. He rolled on his side and saw Eric stumble backward, Jana clutching his ankle with both hands.

Patterson shifted the weapon to aim at Jana, but he never got off the shot. Ryan's bullet caught him square in the chest, sending him crashing backward, down into the shaft, his scream rising over the echo of gunfire.

Ryan crawled to Jana's side. She lay face down on the ground, her shoulders trembling. He gathered her into his arms. "Are you hurt?" he murmured, stroking her hair. "Did he hurt you?"

She raised her head to look at him, tears streaming down her cheeks. "He killed Jenny," she sobbed. "She's down at the bottom of that shaft. He shot her and left her alone down there."

He cradled her head on his shoulder while she sobbed. Nothing he could say would soothe her grief, so he let her cry. When her tears at last subsided, he kissed the top of her head. "I'm glad he didn't kill you, too," he said.

She nodded, and he helped her to stand. "Thank God you came," she said. "I told myself if I could hang on long enough, something would happen. I had to keep trying. I wouldn't give up."

"That's what I love about you." He turned her to him and kissed her again, on the lips. She melted against him, her hands threaded in his hair. It was a kiss of desperation and relief and more than a little passion—emotion heightened, he knew, by all they had been through. But that didn't mean his feelings for her were any less real.

"I know this isn't a good time," he said. "And I'm not asking anything of you. I just want you to know I love you."

"I love you, too," she said. "In spite of everything else, I love you. It's crazy and not at all what I expected, but I can't seem to help myself."

"Police! Ryan? Are you there?" A man's voice echoed off the rock walls of the tunnel.

"We're down here!" Ryan shouted.

Footsteps thundered down the tunnel. Moments later, Ethan, Simon and the rest of the Ranger Brigade appeared in the opening. "Eric Patterson is dead at the bottom of the mine shaft," Ryan said. "Along with Jennifer Lassiter."

"How are you, Officer Spencer?" Graham asked.

"I'm fine now, sir. Just fine." The Rangers stepped aside to let Ryan and Jana pass.

"What happens now?" she asked, when they emerged from the mine.

"I'm taking you home," he said.

"I mean, what happens with Eric, and Jenny?"

"They'll retrieve the bodies. You'll need to decide what to do. If you want a funeral or some kind of memorial service I'll help you with that. Or we can assign you a victim's advocate."

"Poor Jenny." She leaned against him. "If only I had known what she was going through, I could have helped."

"She didn't want to worry you," he said. "And she thought she could handle Eric herself. I talked to Professor Eddleston earlier and he said she liked being with him because he made her feel safe. I think she came on to Eddleston as a way of getting rid of Eric.

She thought if he knew she was involved with someone else, he'd leave her alone."

"He wasn't sane," Jana said. "You heard the way he talked in there—as if Jenny and I were the same person." She raised her head, eyes wide. "I almost forgot—he told me he did murder Lucia and Alicia. And he attacked me that night at Jenny's apartment. He said he did it to practice before he killed Jenny." She covered her mouth with her hand and choked back a fresh sob.

"We'll need a statement from you later," Ryan said. "But not now. You don't have to think about it now."

"I have to tell you before I forget something," she said. "He said he put the shirt in Daniel Metwater's closet, to try to frame him. Oh, and he attacked Andi Mattheson, too, but she got away."

Ryan nodded. So the Rangers had been right to think all these assaults and disappearances were connected. "We'll get your statement tomorrow," he said. "For now, let's get you home."

She studied him. "But your place isn't my home," she said.

"It can be if you want it to be." He led her

around to the passenger side of the car. "Is that what you want?"

"I want to stay with you," she said. "Not just now. I don't want to go back to Denver, except to close out my business there and give up my apartment. I don't want to leave you."

"I want you to stay with me, too." He kissed her again, gently, as if she were made of spun sugar. She seemed so fragile and precious to him now, though he knew she was strong as steel. She had to be, to have endured all she had today.

She smiled through a fresh wave of tears. "Do you think we can make this work?" she asked. "We aren't starting out under the best of circumstances."

"Things will only get better from here," he said. "And whatever happens, we'll get through it together. If that's what you want."

"It's what I want." She threw her arms around him and pulled him close. "I don't give up. You know that, don't you?"

"As long as you don't give up on us."

"Believe it," she said.

"I do." It wasn't a wedding vow, but with luck and time it would be. Now that he had found this woman, he didn't intend to let her go.

* * * * *

*Don't miss the other books in
Cindi Myers's miniseries*
THE RANGER BRIGADE: THE FAMILY
on sale in 2018.

*And be sure to check out
her previous titles in this miniseries:*

*MURDER IN BLACK CANYON
UNDERCOVER HUSBAND*

Available now from Harlequin Intrigue.